He pushed throug█ ████████████████████████ ███ ███
reached down for ██ ████████████████████████████ █
ease him away from the tree, to get ███ ██ ███ ████.
When his hand brushed against the hard shaft of the
arrow, he jumped back as if he had touched a live wire.

When he looked again he could see the arrow deeply
embedded in the red parka just above the top of the
waders. It had entered high and almost exactly in the
center of Rawlings's body.

───────────────── ★ ─────────────────

"Tightly plotted and well-written.... Weber has
'hatched' a compelling tale that will leave readers
guessing until the final pages."
—Tom Eslick, author of *Tracked in the Whites*

Ronald Weber
The
Aluminum
Hatch

TORONTO • NEW YORK • LONDON
AMSTERDAM • PARIS • SYDNEY • HAMBURG
STOCKHOLM • ATHENS • TOKYO • MILAN
MADRID • WARSAW • BUDAPEST • AUCKLAND

THE ALUMINUM HATCH

A Worldwide Mystery/October 1999

First published by Write Way Publishing, Inc.

ISBN 0-373-26324-4

Visit us at www.worldwidemystery.com

Printed in U.S.A.

For Betty and Gordy Morse

ONE

BEING THERE WITH Rawlings gave Mercy the creeps. There was something intimate about the woods, especially now, snow still patching the ground, winter hanging on. She felt like burrowing down in a thicket of balsams, pulling a man after her, waiting for spring.

Being in the woods with winter hanging on was like being in a cut-rate motel off an interstate highway in the middle of the week in a state you were just passing through. Frankly, it made her horny.

Except the man she was with, Rawlings, was the regional director, which meant he was her boss. That wasn't the only thing wrong with him. He was younger than she was—a good half-dozen years, damn it—had three degrees from Michigan State, was attractive in a sandy-haired sort of way, dressed like an Eddie Bauer catalogue, and had the nerve to show her how to do her job.

Which was what he was doing now.

They were crouched thigh-to-thigh in neoprene chest waders on high ground with a view of the river from dense cover of spruce and cedar. The spot was just below Danish Landing, the third access site downriver from Ossning on the mainstream of the Borchard. They would see Link Pickett's canoe when it swept around a bend toward the big cedar stretched nearly across the river.

"You're in charge here," Rawlings was telling her. "Pickett's just another citizen as far as the DNR's concerned."

Mercy sighed. Every now and then a ray of sunlight pierced the clouds and she glanced upward, thankful at least for a hint of changing weather. "It's not that simple, Rawlings. As I've told you."

"What you've told me is the man is out of control. He's a law unto himself."

That's about right, she wanted to say. Instead she said, "He runs a business. There aren't many around here. He makes money, employs people. They like him. Even if they didn't, he'd be a problem. The Picketts are old family in these parts. Lord, Rawlings, they were here with the Ojibways."

She didn't need to look at him to tell Rawlings was shaking his head, sad for her more than irritated. She doubted he was even aware she was a woman—aware beyond the department's affirmative action records. Even if he was inclined to, there wasn't much he could do about a female district officer, Michigan having only a handful. She would have to screw up in a major league way before he could get rid of her. That she was both a woman and competent—such a startling thought wouldn't have crossed his mind.

"Only if you let him, Mercy," Rawlings said, all long-suffering in tone. "You've got to draw a line in the sand with someone like Pickett. Make a stand. He's laughing at you behind your back."

"Yeah, and he's going to be laughing in my face after this."

The plan—Rawlings' plan for her with this outing in the woods—was to start the new season right by putting a stop to Link Pickett's annual clearing of sweepers on the Borchard's mainstream. Winter storms, beavers, gravity, disease, God knew what other natural failings brought the trees down, adding to the river's picturesque appeal while forming new hazards for inexperienced canoeists. Link Pickett liked the river clear. He didn't like his canoes banged up. He didn't like canoeists getting dumped in the river and having to send his people out to bring them back, soaked and grumpy, to the livery in Ossning.

So each spring—meaning in the north woods the handful of days between winter and summer—he put on waders and canoed downstream and cleaned out sweepers. When he came to one, he landed the canoe and got out a chain saw and went to work. People who wintered in cabins along the river knew what was going on when they heard a saw roaring and it made them mad. Usually those people wanted the Borchard left in a natural state, sweepers and all, and even if they didn't they had no love for canoeists who came downriver all summer like a boisterous invasion force, leaving a trail of beer cans and tearing up trout cover.

But if they were old-time residents they knew

better than complain. If they did, things could happen. They could wake up in the middle of the night to shotgun blasts coming out of the woods—and in the morning find a mailbox in pieces or that varnished wood plaque hanging over the front entrance, BEV AND BOB'S HAPPY HAVEN, in splinters.

Newcomers along the river were usually the ones who raised a fuss, complaining to the county commissioners or the Department of Natural Resources. Mercy handled complaints that came to the DNR the same way the commissioners did, by appearing outraged and saying, "I'll look into it. That's for sure." Then all she had to do was drag her feet for a while. She could depend on the same complainants not coming back the following spring.

But this year a complaint had gone directly to the regional office in Traverse City, and the regional office had a new administrator, Rawlings, and he was full of energy and high-minded ambition, a deadly combination. So Mercy was in waders in the woods in April, horny but with a man who gave her the creeps, waiting for Link Pickett to come around the bend to Danish Landing and go to work on the big cedar sweeper. Yesterday his chain saw had been heard upstream. He would be here today.

Rawlings' plan was to wait until Link was up to his waist in water and actually cutting the cedar into the small lengths that could float downriver, before springing out of the woods and making an arrest.

He would have Link red-handed. There would be a stiff fine, a story in the Ossning *Call,* and Rawlings would push for a permanent injunction against further cutting that, if violated, could mean a jail sentence. The community would know that the DNR— the *new* DNR—meant business.

In which case Mercy would have to put in for a transfer. Life would be too complicated in Ossning. The hitch was the town was home and she couldn't imagine leaving the Borchard. And there was Fitzgerald, the newspaperman from Detroit who wanted to marry her. Could she imagine leaving him? She probably should.

She was thinking about that, more or less seriously, when she heard Rawlings suck in his breath. A canoe had swept around the bend.

The downed cedar was still some distance ahead and the canoeist, wearing a baseball cap and leaning forward, rested the paddle across the gunwales. He was making no effort to move in for the bank. The canoe held in the middle of the river, moving swiftly, the water high and fast this time of year, but not discolored. No matter what the run-off from snow or rain the mainstream of the Borchard ordinarily ran clear.

The sun broke through again and for an instant Mercy tilted her face upward. Beside her she felt Rawlings coil, then leap to his feet, and she arose with him, following the angle of his gaze.

The wire stretched tight across the river glistened like silver in the sun.

She gasped, and with Rawlings broke free of spruce and cedar, stood in the clear, and began shouting a warning.

The canoeist seemed about to lift his cap, then at the commotion coming from the high ground suddenly straightened and looked to the side, toward them, his face uplifted.

It was at this moment that the current shot him, at a point located just beneath his chin, into the lethal wire strung across the stream.

TWO

OSSNING'S BUSINESS DISTRICT was a single street of a half-dozen blocks with the city-county building anchoring one end and the community hospital the other. A highway intersected the street exactly in the middle, the road running north to the Mackinac Bridge and the Upper Peninsula, with motels and gas stations and government agencies strung out along its length before giving way to a vista of jackpine barrens. A hotel, square, four stories, bricks painted a peeling earth-red, occupied one corner of the downtown intersection.

Fitzgerald wasn't fond of Ossning in summer, tourists everywhere, too many stopping to eat in the cafés on the main drag or poke through the antique and trinket shops. The hotel, on the other hand, was largely ignored. Tourists found something forbidding about an old hotel in the center of town, assuming it housed derelicts or north woods whores, and passed it up in favor of the highway motels. It was a view Fitzgerald encouraged whenever he had the opportunity. Before he found a place to rent on the river he lived a couple weeks in the hotel and learned to like it the way it was, old, shabby, no derelicts or whores in residence but with the best food in town.

He preferred Ossning in winter, tourists and summer residents gone, snow banked high along the curbs, some businesses shut down, the owners basking in Florida along with half the population of Michigan.

In late afternoon, just before the northern dark settled in, he parked his Grand Cherokee—spanking new, one of his splurges—in front of the hotel and hurried inside.

Like most northern places, the hotel was overheated and he had to peel off layers of clothing. But the warmth was pleasant when he got used to it and the soft lighting was just right and the bar was long and polished and had good padded stools.

Before, dreaming about winter in the north, he saw himself in a cabin on the river, wood fire roaring in a big stone fireplace, tying flies and reading Thoreau and maybe working on his novel, all the while sipping whiskey through the long night. Instead, he drove to town in the late afternoon, blinding snowstorms excepted, and settled into the cozy cocoon of the hotel bar and drank schooners of beer while he listened to Nils and talked with the locals and waited for Mercy Virdon to finish work.

He had never heard anyone use Nils' last name. A Finn who lived back in the pines in a mobile home, Nils came to town most nights and played the accordion for the diners in the hotel in return for a meal and all the schooners of beer he could drink. Nils was in his seventies, Fitzgerald guessed, and his girlfriend, Wilma, was probably the same.

Wilma sat in the bar while Nils played. Between sets she drank with him and the two of them talked in low tones.

About nine o'clock, the last diners gone and waitresses setting the tables for the next day, Nils and Wilma left the hotel together and vanished into the icy dark. Fitzgerald and Mercy usually did the same, heading out for his rented A-frame on the river at Walther Bridge.

This night, a promise of spring in the air, the heat in the hotel was more intense than usual. Fitzgerald said hello to Sandy, the frizzy-haired brunette bartender, then peeled down to his bottom layer of shirts, an old blue button-down from his working days, and tucked the tails into his corduroys.

Nils was playing "My Funny Valentine" in the dining room as he took the bar stool next to Wilma. She gave Fitzgerald a wink of greeting, eyes encircled with greenish shadow, but said nothing. Nils, perched on the edge of a wood stool, played with his eyes closed, which Fitzgerald thought might be a defense against the fact that most of the diners kept right on talking through his set. He went from one song to another, all old favorites, playing them by heart. Fitzgerald didn't have much feeling for accordion music but he liked to watch Nils, dressed in the shiny gray suit he always wore, hair coal-black despite his age and flattened back from his forehead, perched on his stool at the head of the room, eyes closed, stubbornly playing his songs.

When Nils finished he unstrapped the accordion,

left it beside the stool, and headed for a place at the bar beside Wilma. Every diner in the place knew him but nobody said a thing as he passed by, slapping him on the back and telling him what a fine fellow he was or requesting a song. And there wasn't a big brandy glass somewhere that diners could stuff with dollar bills. In the north woods there weren't many spare dollar bills, and everyone knew Nils wouldn't have taken them if there were. Finns like Nils would accept a meal and let Sandy draw him a beer in return for entertaining with the accordion, but you wouldn't think of giving him a tip.

Nils drank off half a schooner before he looked beyond Wilma at Fitzgerald.

"Spring's in the air," Fitzgerald said. "You can feel it."

"The hell."

"You can't feel it?"

"Too damn early."

Finns living back in the woods through the winter tended to become morose. Ordinarily it was a quality Fitzgerald didn't care for, and it was one he hadn't found in Thoreau. Thoreau could be tedious but he was never morose. On the other hand, Ossning wasn't exactly Concord and Thoreau didn't have to play the accordion for food and drink in a hotel dining room and when he wrote *Walden* he wasn't seventy-plus years old. Fitzgerald had come to like Nils even though he was a morose Finn, but

tonight, the weather beginning to shift, he wanted
to lighten his mood. He asked Nils about the Tigers.

"No guys to pitch."

"They can hit," Fitzgerald said. "It could carry
them."

"Naw. They fold the tent by the Fourth of July."

Fitzgerald smiled. He could usually get Nils talking about baseball, that leading to other things. The
best was what Nils remembered about Ossning
from the past. He could remember when lumbering
was still big business in the woods and there were
grayling left in the cold feeder creeks of the Borchard and auto executives came by train from Detroit to fish and stay in private sporting clubs.

Wilma, sitting between them, said nothing. She
talked with Nils when the two of them were alone,
and she would talk with Fitzgerald and with Mercy
Virdon, but she wouldn't say a word while the two
men were talking together. Wilma was a woman of
the old school.

"You done tying?" Fitzgerald asked.

It was another subject that usually worked.
Through the winter Nils and Wilma tied flies for
Link Pickett, who ran a shop called The Tackle Box
at his canoe livery. Because of his eyes Nils was
limited to big flies, mostly gray and brown drakes
and the Hexagenia. His Hex flies were considered
classics, but there were some fishermen who
thought Wilma was even better with the pattern
than Nils. For his part Fitzgerald couldn't tell their
work apart. Couldn't yet. He figured he would need

a second lifetime on the Borchard to get to that point.

"The hell," Nils said, glowering into his beer.

"You haven't finished?" As far as Fitzgerald knew, filling orders from Link Pickett for opening day of the fishing season was the main source of income for Nils and Wilma, beside whatever Uncle Sam doled out in Social Security.

"Finished good as damned hell."

That seemed rather definite, causing Fitzgerald to take a closer look at Nils. His eyes were dark, deep-set, maybe more morose than usual. His forehead was furrowed with thought. "You want a shot with the beer?" Fitzgerald asked. "Help us think spring." He was about to signal Sandy when Nils shook his head.

"No?"

"Give me some numbers instead."

"Ah, Nils," Fitzgerald sighed.

"We'll beat the bastard."

"You know the odds?" Fitzgerald tried to explain. "You've got a better chance of drowning in your bathtub than winning the Michigan lottery. And winning twice—they probably can't even calculate the odds on something like that."

"A cop in Livonia," Nils said, "he beat the bastard three times. It was in the *Call*."

"There's another thing. I give you some numbers, you don't win, which you won't, and it's my fault. You'll blame me."

"Naw," Nils said, and shuffled through his vest

pocket for a scrap of paper for Fitzgerald to write on. "I never do that."

DURING NILS' next set Fitzgerald got another schooner of beer for himself and one for Wilma and they had a quiet conversation. Fitzgerald pointed out that winning a state lottery wasn't all it was cracked up to be. For one thing, the money came in over a twenty-year period and the federal government took its cut each year. You didn't end up with that much real dough. It wasn't exactly the pot of gold everyone thought.

Wilma smiled a lot while he talked, a line of beer foam glistening above two slashes of fiery lipstick. She was too polite to ask how much he had actually won in the lottery, and so was Nils. On the other hand, they probably already knew. Fitzgerald had told Verlyn Kelso when he came up to the river, needing Verlyn's help in finding a place to rent and having to explain why he wanted it for a full year, and now everyone in town knew. He might as well have put a notice in the *Call*. Another mistake was telling Verlyn he was thinking of writing a novel while he was living on the river. Now everyone thought of him as the book writer from Detroit who won the state lottery.

He hadn't won one of the mammoth jackpots but a smaller one, two million. Half was settled on his wife right away, the financial ground of an amicable divorce, then he had taken an indefinite leave of absence from the *Free Press* and gone to the north

woods with an income of thirty-six grand a year for
two decades. He was hardly wealthy, and when you
factored in inflation his long-term situation wasn't
so great. But it was a nice little annuity, no denying
that. He was one of the better-healed people in the
chronically depressed north.

But it was the luck more than the money that
interested people. The money was his, the luck
might be transferred. If you touched him it might
rub off. People in the north woods didn't do a lot
of touching, not in public, so the next best thing
was to get his numbers. Some luck might rub off
on them. When Fitzgerald went into his story about
the odds and dying in your bathtub people agreed
with him, then asked for his numbers anyway.

He wrote some out for Wilma on another scrap
of paper, the first numbers that came into his head,
pure free association, and she thanked him and put
the paper in her purse. Then she told him what Nils
had meant about Link Pickett. Why she and Nils
were finished tying for him.

"Jesus," Fitzgerald said, "Link's dead?"

Wilma repeated it and Fitzgerald stared at her.
Wilma looked back at him with blank, green-
rimmed eyes. "I told Nils we got to get on tying
with Verlyn."

"That's not going to be easy," Fitzgerald found
himself saying. "You know how Verlyn feels. I
stopped in at Link's place once and bought some
tippet material. Two spools—maybe six bucks in
all. When Verlyn got wind of it he wouldn't speak

to me for a week." He could hear the sound of his voice, talking calmly with Wilma, and couldn't believe it. "I don't know, Wilma. That you tied for Link could be trouble."

"I told Nils we got to do something new for Verlyn. Maybe some good drakes. He already knows the Hex pattern."

"Everybody knows your Hex, Wilma."

"But Nils says no. He says Verlyn won't buy nothing. It won't matter how good."

"Really?" Fitzgerald said. Then, finally, he was able to stop the flow of his talk. "*Dead,* Wilma?"

"Took his head right off," Wilma said.

FITZGERALD DIDN'T GET the full story until Nils finished his set and returned to the bar and Sandy pulled him another beer. Link Pickett, out on the mainstream of the Borchard for his annual clearing of sweepers, had run into a wire strung across the river at Danish Landing. The wire, set at just the right height for a canoeist, had caught Link in the throat. Since he was moving fast, the river high, he had been nearly decapitated.

"Shoulda been done before," Nils said.

"Jesus, Nils."

"He was one big bastard."

"Even so."

"Except he paid good."

"So does Verlyn," Fitzgerald said, then added the kicker you always had to add when talking about Verlyn Kelso, "if you cut a deal."

"Goddamn Verlyn to hell."

Fitzgerald waited before he said, "I don't get it, Nils."

Nils looked at him like he was dead between the ears. "You don't buy no flies from prison."

"*Verlyn* did it?"

"Who the hell you think?"

"Any fisherman on the Borchard. Anyone who hates canoeists. Me, for instance. Or Calvin McCann."

"Calvin's down there in New Zealand."

"I heard he's back." Then Fitzgerald said, "Jesus, Nils. Mercy could have done it. She always had some trouble going with Link."

A mournful look came into Nils' eyes, replacing moroseness. The look suggested that Fitzgerald's ignorance was invincible. "Naw," he said with a tired effort at explanation. "Mercy's the one fished him out the river."

"What?"

"You seen she ain't here tonight? She's at the jail is why."

THREE

THE TAMARACK COUNTY sheriff, Willard Stroud, had just finished briefing two reporters, an anorexic-thin blond from the television station in Traverse City and Gus Thayer of the *Call,* when Fitzgerald appeared in his office.

"You working now?" Stroud asked him.

Fitzgerald said, "No, nothing's changed. I'm just looking for Mercy."

Stroud said, "Wait a minute," and handled two more questions from the reporters. "It's way too early in the investigation," he told them, "to say anything definite."

Then he took Fitzgerald down a hallway to a small lounge where Mercy Virdon and the DNR man, Rawlings, were sipping coffee from styrofoam containers and looking over printouts of the statements they had given earlier.

Was it really true, Stroud wondered, that Fitzgerald wasn't working? He looked the way Stroud thought Detroit newspapermen ought to look—unruly dark hair that needed cutting, bushy black mustache, the type who looked disheveled no matter what he wore—but Fitzgerald claimed he was on leave of absence or something, living out on the river so he could fish all summer and tie flies all winter. That wasn't surprising. Trout bums from Chicago and Detroit and Cleveland showed up on the river now and then and stuck it out about a year before they went off to Montana or Colorado or New Mexico, trying the latest hot spots there.

But Stroud hadn't run into one before who was a newspaperman.

When he learned that was Fitzgerald's occupation he made a point of having a talk with him. He didn't want to be blind-sided one morning by a story in the Detroit paper written by somebody who was supposed to be a trout bum. One night in July he stayed out fishing the Hex hatch on the South Branch of the Borchard, and afterward he stopped at the Black Duck in Kinnich for an early breakfast. All the trout bums, fishing late when the Hex was on, ended up at the Black Duck before dawn, and they were inclined to talk after nothing all night but seeing inky dark all around them and hearing big browns slurp bugs.

When Fitzgerald showed up in the restaurant Stroud introduced himself and they swapped lies for a while about monster fish they had hooked but hadn't been able to net. Stroud liked him, and he liked fishing talk, but that wasn't the point of the conversation. "I hear you work for the *Free Press,*" he said finally.

"You've got good sources," Fitzgerald said.

Stroud shrugged. "A small place like this, you don't have to try. You hear things. You know how it is."

"I'm learning," Fitzgerald said, and gave Stroud a broad smile. Then he dug out his wallet and showed his press card. "I covered local politics for the paper, which in Detroit meant I played second-fiddle to the sports desk. Then I came into some money and split with my wife and decided to take a long vacation. I want to spend a full year, all the seasons, living on the Borchard."

"What for?" Stroud asked.

"Good question," Fitzgerald said, and lapsed into silence. He seemed to be thinking his answer through. Then he said, "Before, coming up to fish, I'd stay two or three days at best. I'd camp or sleep in the car or take a motel if the weather went bad. I kept seeing the river in bits and pieces. My experience, it was like a bunch of snapshots, no order to them. I kept wondering what it was like up here all the time, seeing how the seasons developed, getting some continuity in my life. You ever read Thoreau?"

Stroud shrugged. "Heard of him."

"One of the things I like about *Walden* is it treats a whole year. Actually, Thoreau was at the pond two years but he only wrote about the first."

"Interesting," Stroud said.

"So that's it. Why I'm up here."

"You're a writer, too."

"Newspaper writer," Fitzgerald corrected him.

"The other kind. Books."

"A story that's gotten around," Fitzgerald said. "I'd like to write a novel, is all."

"And you won the lottery."

Fitzgerald smiled again, a little less broad. "Not the big one."

"None of my business," Stroud said.

"I'm self-supporting. I won't be on county relief."

"Like I say," Stroud said. "None of my business."

He didn't want to get personal. He just wanted Fitzgerald to know he kept an ear to the ground. He made the round of the coffee shops and saloons in the county, listening more than he talked, picking up the gossip. He liked to know what might happen before it happened. Nothing changed because of that; things happened anyway. But it made him feel more comfortable if he'd seen them coming.

Stroud talked some more with Fitzgerald that morning in the Black Duck and when they left they said they would see each other on the river. That happened a couple times. He also ran into Fitzgerald in Ossning and they exchanged a few words. He saw people ask Fitzgerald for lottery numbers and Fitzgerald obliged.

Once, meeting again in the Black Duck in Kinnich, Stroud asked Fitzgerald if he had ever considered writing fishing articles. "For magazines," Stroud said. "*Field and Stream, Outdoor Life*. That sort of thing."

"Thought about it," Fitzgerald said.

"You like to fish—you're a writer. You could do it."

"Actually, I talked about it once with Calvin. He didn't think it was a good idea."

"Calvin McCann?"

"Calvin's view is that ninety-nine percent of what you read in fishing articles is pure bunk. No fisherman tells the truth about good fishing holes or hot flies, let alone tells it to the world. So, in the articles, writers make everything up. Reading fishing articles you're really reading short stories."

"Calvin's a crank."

"Anyway," Fitzgerald said, "I decided to write fiction and call it that. Try to write it. I'm not making much headway."

Stroud had heard that Mercy Virdon had moved in with Fitzgerald in the place he was renting at Walther Bridge. It was set in heavy timber above the river, a cedar-sided A-frame with a big stone fireplace that had been built by a GM executive as a summer home. A year or two after the executive moved in he was downsized and the Old Kent Bank took possession and rented it to Fitzgerald. That was the sort of information Stroud kept up on. He stored it away in his head, dormant, until it was needed.

Now it might be.

The A-frame was just downriver from Kelso's Kabin Kamp. Fitzgerald and Verlyn Kelso were virtual neighbors. And there was the fact that Mercy and Verlyn had been married once and had a boy, Kit, who kept them connected. As Stroud added it all up, there was a possibility that Fitzgerald would

get involved, and that meant he could have a Detroit newspaperman nosing around.

Trout bums he could handle. About Detroit
newspapermen he had enough sense to have his
doubts.

MERCY LOOKED AT HIM when Fitzgerald came in
the lounge, then went back to reading her statement.
Stroud couldn't detect anything in the look. A faded
blond, over forty by now, Mercy was always hard
to read. Her eyes, light blue and set wide apart,
could seem dead serious one moment, amused the
next. He could never get a fix on what was going
on inside her head, if anything was.

Rawlings either didn't know Fitzgerald or
couldn't be deflected from his statement. He was
hunched over the paper, absorbed, moving a ball-
point pen from line to line. "This is Fitzgerald,"
Mercy said to him.

Rawlings glanced up then, took in all he wanted
to take in, and returned to the statement. Rawlings
might not know Fitzgerald, Stroud decided, but he
had heard of him.

"Look," Rawlings said, "about the wire."

"We can go back to the office," Stroud said.

Rawlings waved a hand in Fitzgerald's direction,
indicating that his presence didn't matter. "I want
you to understand. It was a dangerous situation. I
responded instinctively."

Stroud thought for a moment. He didn't want to
make a fuss about Fitzgerald being present, stir

things up when there wasn't any need. If Fitzgerald was going to be around, and he probably was because of Mercy, he wanted to keep things cordial between them as long as he could. That seemed the best strategy.

He looked at Rawlings and said, "That's what the statement says."

"It's not that. It's what you said before."

"You tampered with evidence. You went banging through the woods, released the wire, messed up anything that might have been around. Maybe some footprints. We don't know what might have been there. DNR, you ought to know better. That's what I said."

Taking a shot at the DNR was hard to resist. If Fitzgerald did write something about Link Pickett's murder for the Detroit paper Stroud hoped he would get that in. When the DNR meddled in law enforcement it always got things wrong. Its job was to watch out for the environment, and it usually got that wrong, too. Stroud had come to an accommodation with Mercy, meaning that she had learned to keep out of his way and he kept out of hers. As far as he could tell, Mercy's boss from Traverse City hadn't learned anything.

"Try to understand," Rawlings said patiently. "Mercy and I managed to get Pickett's body to the bank. When we saw nothing could be done, she stayed there and I followed the wire across the river. I couldn't leave it that way. My action was instinctive. Another canoeist might have come down the river.''

"So you could have released one end of the wire. Why the hell both?''

Rawlings sighed. "I realize in retrospect that was a mistake.''

"Your next one. You shouldn't have touched the wire at all. After you called in on the car phone you and Mercy should have stayed in the river at the wire in case anyone came down. No one else would this time of year.''

"One couldn't be certain.''

"One could if one had called me first,'' Stroud said, getting as much edge in his voice as possible. "I'd of told you.''

"All right,'' Rawlings said. "We agree to disagree.''

"No we don't. You were wrong.''

Rawlings rolled his eyes, shook his head, sighed again. Stroud waited him out, then said, "Something else bothering you?''

"What I meant to say is the whole matter seems academic. You already have your man.''

Stroud narrowed his eyes. He wasn't sure he wanted Fitzgerald to hear what might be coming. "You must know something I don't.''

"Only what Mercy told me. It sounded conclusive.''

"Mercy doesn't happen to be the sheriff here,'' Stroud said. "I don't recall Tamarack County electing her to anything. And there's something called proof. Proof is conclusive."

"Have it your way," Rawlings said, and went back to reading his statement, moving the pen line by line. When he was done, he signed the statement and stood up. Stroud told him he would want to talk again, tomorrow probably, to see if Rawlings recalled anything else. In the meantime Rawlings should say nothing to the newspaper or television people. All inquiries should be directed to the sheriff's office.

Rawlings said, "You understand, of course, that Mercy and I must make internal reports. We were engaged in a DNR operation."

"Send me copies."

"That really isn't required, sheriff. We were acting within our jurisdiction."

"Don't argue," Stroud said.

"SOMETHING BOTHERING YOU, too?" Stroud asked after Rawlings left.

"No," Mercy said, and signed her statement.

"Now let's talk off the record."

"About what?"

"You know what. You seem to think the case is open and shut."

"I don't think anything," Mercy said. "I just told Rawlings what everybody knows. What you know. Verlyn's been threatening Link Pickett for years. I shouldn't have said it."

"Why did you?"

"I don't know," Mercy said. "I had to say something—try to offer an explanation. It was a damned bloody mess out there."

"And you and Rawlings messed it up all the more."

"We've been over that. What he said is the way it happened. His first thought was to release the wire so nothing else would happen. He didn't think about trampling evidence. There probably wouldn't have been any evidence anyway."

Stroud waited, letting some time pass. At moments like this he wished he hadn't given up smoking. Getting out a pack of cigarettes, shaking one loose, lighting up, exhaling a long line of smoke... It made for effective pauses when you were handling a case and weren't sure yet where to go with it.

"Verlyn's too smart to leave a trail. That's what you think?"

"What I think," Mercy said carefully, "is that he had nothing to do with it. He'd know that if anything happened to Link Pickett he'd be a suspect. Vice versa, for that matter. They were public enemies, Stroud. You know that. They've been painting themselves into a corner for years. All they could do was talk."

"That isn't what you told Rawlings."

"I've explained that," Mercy sighed. "I said Verlyn *threatened* Link. I didn't mean he *killed* him."

"All right," Stroud said. "So what you're telling me is Verlyn has an alibi?"

"In a way."

"On the other hand," Stroud said, "maybe that's what he wants us to think. Everyone would suspect him if anything happened to Link, so it couldn't be him. He wouldn't risk it. Verlyn might have figured it out that way."

"He's not that smart."

"No?" Stroud said, and smiled at her. "How come you married him then?"

"Very funny," Mercy said.

WHILE MERCY gathered her things to leave, Stroud had a moment alone with Fitzgerald.

"What I said to Mercy applies to you. Everything you heard is off the record."

"I'm not working," Fitzgerald said.

"In case you change your mind. I'd like to know that ahead of time."

"Depend on it."

Stroud nodded and shifted the subject. "How well have you gotten to know Verlyn Kelso? Living where you do on the river, you're almost neighbors."

"We see each other. I go in the fly shop."

"You like him?"

"I'm an outsider up here. I try to like everyone."

"Verlyn's a royal shit. So was Link Pickett. I could tell you some stories."

"I'm sure you could."

"You heard Verlyn threaten Link?"

"Who hasn't?"

"You see what I mean? Even an outsider knows that."

"Look," Fitzgerald said. "I've been around here long enough to know that every fisherman on the river wanted Link Pickett out of business. He had plenty of enemies."

"True," Stroud said. "But Verlyn was at the top of the list."

Then Stroud took a small spiral notebook out of his shirt pocket and unclipped a ball-point pen. He had done Fitzgerald a favor, letting him listen in while he talked with Rawlings and Mercy. He hadn't tried to freeze him out because he was a Detroit newspaperman who might decide to go back to work. He had treated him like someone who had a relationship with Mercy and so had a reason to be involved in the case. Fitzgerald, the point was, owed him a little something in return.

"You wouldn't mind putting down a few numbers," he said, "I'd appreciate it."

STROUD WENT BACK to his office after he finished with Mercy and Fitzgerald.

"You've got a visitor waiting on you," a deputy told him. "Link's brother. Mad as hell."

"Well?" Brand Pickett demanded the moment Stroud entered the office. "You got him locked up?"

"I take it," Stroud said as calmly as he could, "you have someone in mind."

"The one who did it," Brand said fiercely. "Verlyn Kelso."

FOUR

THE LOW SLANT of morning light turned the Clutha's surface into blinking diamonds. Before the day's warmth settled into the high valley the air was clean and sharp. At this altitude South Island mornings were always cold, emptying the mind, filling him with anticipation. Calvin had gotten the gear arranged, strung the rods, picked out big attractor flies to start with, got the two American business tycoons settled at the head of good runs.

They were on their own now. He was going fishing himself.

Eight hours stretched ahead in the valley before the helicopter swept them back to the angling hotel at Slowdne—eight hours in which they wouldn't see another fisherman on the Clutha and would land so many three-and four-pound browns they could stop counting. Before he went in the water he would gather driftwood for a fire on a rocky bar at the river's edge. For an hour or so he would cast, then come back and boil a pot of coffee and warm fresh-baked cinnamon rolls and call in the two tycoons for a morning snack. It was how he kept them happy.

Then he would get in two more hours of casting before he grilled trout for lunch and opened a bottle

of local chardonnay. That always impressed the tycoons. They didn't know New Zealand produced
good wine. Calvin didn't touch the stuff himself but
he had heard it praised. He thought it might only
be the air and the river and the high mountain valley adding to the taste. Everything tasted good out
here.

He was about to take his first step in the Clutha,
rod in hand and reading the surface of the water
ahead, when the phone rang.

It took a while to come up out of sleep, leaving
South Island back in his dream and realizing where
he was. Then it took him a while to remember the
telephone was on the wall in the kitchen. The cabin
felt strange. It always did after he got back. He was
still getting books unpacked and setting out tying
materials on the long table by the wood-burning
stove. The place wouldn't feel right until he had
everything arranged. The phone was on about its
tenth ring when he answered.

"Thank goodness!"

Calvin said, "Laurel?"

"I thought you weren't there."

"Where would I be?" Then he said, "What time
is it?"

"It's late, but I have to see you. Please."

He switched on the kitchen light with his free
hand and looked at the clock above the refrigerator.
It wasn't late, ten-forty, but Laurel knew guides
turned in early and rose early. It was a bad habit of

the trade. He couldn't shake it even when he wasn't working.

She was talking fast about Link and he couldn't take it all in. "Mellow out," he said. There was silence on the other end of the line then, an unnatural silence, and Calvin felt his body tense. He was suddenly wide awake. He could hear Laurel taking long gulps of air, choking back something.

"You okay?"

"Link's dead."

"What?"

"Murdered, Calvin."

Then her voice changed. She wasn't gulping air now but releasing it, settling into something, perfectly calm. "I remembered you don't watch the news. It was on the TV but you wouldn't know."

"I read," Calvin said. "You don't learn anything important from the tube."

"You would have learned Link was dead."

Calvin didn't have a response to that but it didn't matter. Laurel was doing the talking. "That's why we can see each other. We don't have a thing to worry about in the world."

CALVIN HAD BEEN back in Michigan less than a week and this would be the third time he had been with Laurel Pickett. It was always sweet and they both had a lot of stored-up feeling and he liked the danger involved. His lady in New Zealand, Patty Dunvoold, was a divorcee with two teenage children and there was no danger being with her.

Laurel wasn't just another married woman in a small town in the north woods where everyone knew everyone else's business. She was the wife of the sonofabitch who ran canoes on the Borchard's mainstream and had done as much harm to the river as the lumbermen who first cut the old-growth pine and let the sunlight in that raised the water temperature and floated logs that scoured the banks and silted up the streambed.

The aluminum hatch.

That was what Verlyn Kelso called the first warm days of summer when the canoes emerged like an insect hatch and started coming downriver from Ossning and screwed up the fishing for the rest of the year, leaving only early morning and late evening when, if you were wading the river, they weren't bearing down on you. Calvin only guided trips for Kelso's Kabin Kamp on the South Branch, the last part of the Borchard that was still remote and wild and free of canoes except for the fishermen who floated the river. If someone started running pleasure canoes on the South Branch he planned to look for summer work in the Upper Peninsula or out in Montana.

Laurel Pickett was a good-looking woman and she knew her way around the river, but he probably wouldn't have kept it going with her this long if she wasn't Link's wife. Meeting her out at the Keg O'Nails didn't have an effect on the aluminum hatch but it made Calvin feel better about it. Link controlled the canoes on the Borchard but he couldn't control his wife.

There was satisfaction in knowing that.

He put on jeans and a chamois-cloth shirt and a wool shirt over that. In the bathroom he examined his beard in the mirror, thought it could stand some trimming, instead ran a comb through it and pulled his hair back into a ponytail and clamped it with a leather thong. Both, beard and ponytail, seemed more gray than when he last looked. He put on his metal-rimmed tying glasses and had a closer look. It was hard to tell and didn't make any difference anyway.

Gray hair made a guide look like he knew more.

THE HEADLIGHTS from his pickup cut through the long tunnel of jack pine that led from the cabin along a dead end dirt road to the highway into Ossning. Calvin was in a hurry but he drove carefully, alert for deer springing out of the woods at this time of night. From town he would take the highway west in the direction of Traverse City. On the phone, Laurel had said she could come to his place. It would be quicker, and now, given what had happened to Link, they didn't need to worry about being seen together.

"Hell we don't," Calvin told her. "Think about it."

Laurel had described how Link had been killed, and that was all Willard Stroud would need to know. Verlyn might as well have left his signature at the scene. Taking Link out with an arrow would be the only thing more obvious. Proving Verlyn did it would be Stroud's problem. Verlyn had a loud mouth, but he was no dummy. He had probably planned it all winter and done it carefully and hadn't left any incriminating evidence behind. It had been a clean kill, assuming Laurel had the story straight, and Calvin had to admire Verlyn for carrying it off. He himself had never thought seriously about killing Link. He had gone after his wife instead.

Therein was the potential problem.

If Willard Stroud couldn't prove anything about Verlyn, he would start looking around for someone else. He couldn't have a big businessman like Link Pickett with his head sliced off and nobody to put away for it. It wouldn't take him long to find out what Laurel had been doing out at the Keg O'Nails—and who she had been doing it with. Stroud might know already. The only precautions Calvin had taken were that Laurel didn't come to his cabin on the river and he didn't come to her house in town. Unless they were really anxious about covering their tracks and drove to Traverse City, the Keg O'Nails was the place most people in Ossning went when they were fooling around with someone else's wife or husband. Calvin had half hoped Link would catch on and come looking for him to have it out, man to man.

If that had happened, Calvin might have had to think seriously about killing Link.

THE KEG O'NAILS was set in a hacked-out opening in the pine barrens, a log bar and restaurant with an orange neon sign on the roof and a log motel out behind. From the highway you could see the bar and restaurant but you couldn't see the crushed-stone parking lot or the motel. Laurel's Bronco was in the lot, parked off at the edge beside a wall of pine and away from other vehicles located around the lot.

Calvin pulled the pickup in beside her and rolled down the window. He wanted to make sure she only wanted to talk. It wouldn't look right if the two of them headed off to the motel so soon after Link was killed. But he didn't have a chance to open his mouth before Laurel said, "God, I need a beer."

At night, the Keg O'Nails was a hangout for kids, jukebox roaring, air thick with cigarette smoke and the smell of frying hamburgers and spilled beer. Calvin tried not to breathe in the smoke or the smells and pushed through the kids to the bar and got two cans of Stroh's Light for Laurel and a pair of O'Doul's nonalcoholic for him, and pushed back out of the place as quick as he could. He was aware of some kids looking at him and grinning, but he didn't have time to deal with that.

He got in the Bronco beside Laurel and pulled open a beer and handed it to her. She took a long drink, then leaned back against the door, eyes closed. "Tell me again," Calvin said. "Go slow."

She repeated the story. "Mercy Virdon and a

DNR man from Traverse City, Mercy's boss, were out at Danish Landing and saw the whole thing. They were eyewitnesses. Afterward, Mercy waited with Link's body while her boss called for an ambulance. There wasn't anything they could do. He was dead already.''

"That's strange," Calvin said, "Mercy being there.''

"I suppose.''

"Why was she?''

Laurel shrugged and said, "She just was.''

Calvin nodded. Some things defied explanation. Then he said to Laurel, "You're a widow now.''

"It hasn't sunk in yet.''

"You seen the body?''

Laurel grimaced. "God, no.''

"You'll have to.''

"Why?''

"Everyone knew Link, but Willard Stroud will want an official identification.''

"Brand did it. He's the one Stroud called first. Brand came over to the house with Tyler and Tyler's wife.''

"That's good.''

"Stroud thought it was better for family to break the news.''

Calvin thought for a while before he asked, "Who's Tyler, exactly?''

"Link's uncle, the one in the septic tank business.''

"I remember now. How's Brand taking the news?"

"How do you think? Stroud told him to leave Verlyn alone and keep his mouth shut in town. Brand said he would if Stroud put Verlyn behind bars. Otherwise he'd take care of things himself."

"Brand's a hothead."

"He's got reason," Laurel said. "God, I can hardly believe it."

"You know," Calvin said, trying to be helpful, "the funeral people will fix Link up. You won't notice a thing."

He was about to tell her about a friend of his who'd been wiped out on a Harley-Davidson and then fixed up for the casket nearly as good as new. But on second thought he let it pass. He gave Laurel time to drink more beer and get a cigarette out of her purse and light up. He rolled down the window beside him even though the night was cold. A woman who smoked had to be pretty good to keep his interest. Patty Dunvoold was and so was Laurel. Her hair was a shade of red and cut short and in the light from the neon sign on the Keg O'Nails he could see the gleam of her lipstick and smell the heavy scent of her perfume. He couldn't see her shape, hidden under a winter parka, but he didn't need to. He knew it was there.

"You going to take over the business?" he asked after a while.

"Think I ought to?"

"Junk those goddamn canoes. That's what I think."

"You've got canoes."

"For guiding, not pleasure. There's a difference."

"Anyway, somebody else would start up a business. People want to canoe down the river."

"Rivers are for fishing."

"Not *just* fishing." Then Laurel said, "Brand offered to buy out Link's half of the business if I wanted. Right after he told me about Link. He didn't even wait."

"Somebody should have taken out Brand while they were at it."

"Somebody?" Laurel said sharply. "You know who killed Link."

Calvin sipped his O'Doul's and waited a minute or two before he said, "I know who *talked* about killing Link."

"It's the same thing," Laurel said. "That's what I told Willard Stroud when he talked to me. Exactly the same thing."

"How do you figure?" Calvin said. "Link had enemies other than Verlyn Kelso. Hell, there's even Mercy Virdon."

"No," Laurel said firmly.

"Because she was there when it happened? She could have strung the wire before."

"I told you. It wasn't Mercy."

"Okay," Calvin said, "mellow out." Then he

said, "I had something going with his wife. I could have killed Link."

"That's why I had to see you tonight."

"Sure. Because of what happened."

"I had to make certain."

Calvin stroked his beard and peered at her across the seat of the Bronco. "About what?"

"You know."

"Come on, Laurel."

"That you didn't kill Link and make it look like Verlyn did it."

"Shit, Laurel."

"Because you wanted us to be together and Link was in the way and you thought about it down in New Zealand all winter and so you did it right away when you got back."

"We were together already."

"Married, I meant."

"I didn't kill Link."

"I'd understand if you had."

"Get it straight," Calvin said. "I didn't."

Laurel handed him the empty beer can and he opened another for her and another O'Doul's for himself, then waited while she lit another stinking cigarette.

"It's a relief to know," she said, but the tone of her voice suggested the news hadn't exactly come as a surprise. Calvin had the impression Laurel knew all along he hadn't killed Link. Then why had she even raised the possibility? As far as there was any answer at all, he put it down to the strange nature of married women.

"We never talked about getting married anyway," he said.

"We can now."

"We will," he promised her. Then he said, "C'mon, Laurel. You didn't really think I killed Link."

"It would have been something if you had. It would have told me how you felt. About us."

Calvin looked away, out the front of the Bronco toward the motel. No lights showed in any of the rooms. People who used the motel didn't spend a lot of time reading or watching television. Vehicles around the parking area were dark as well, the people inside having little need of light, either.

"You already know how I feel."

"I hope so."

To change the subject Calvin said, "It doesn't look good for Verlyn."

"I hope he rots in everlasting hell."

Laurel's vehemence surprised him and he turned and stared at her. "It's got to be proved first," he found himself saying. "Verlyn's not stupid. He could have covered his tracks."

"Then I hope Brand does what he said."

Calvin tried to think up something more in defense of Verlyn, but before he could Laurel added, "Takes off his head just like Link's."

FIVE

CALL ME—LUNCH.

Fitzgerald read the scrawled note beside the coffee-maker, wondered how Mercy had showered, made breakfast, and left the house without his hearing a sound. Then he filled a mug with coffee and followed a rectangle of sunshine from the kitchen across plank flooring to the glass-walled front of the A-frame.

The day was bright and clear, the season turning. He held the thought in his head even after he stepped outside on the deck and felt the sharp cold of the morning and looked down through the tops of spruce and cedar at the heavy black flow of the river. It was trapped in shade, the sun not yet high enough to touch it. Mounds of crusted snow were still visible along the bank. But the morning would warm and the river with it. He had been right the day before: spring was in the air.

A lake is the landscape's most beautiful and expressive feature. Thoreau got that wrong. A river is.

Yesterday, following Mercy's DNR Suburban back from Ossning, he hadn't been thinking about the weather. He had suggested a drink at the hotel after they left the sheriff's office, but Mercy shook her head and said she just wanted to go home. He could see she was exhausted, and with good reason. He pondered a strategy. Should he try to get her to talk about what had happened at Danish Landing, all the gory details, or should he leave it alone, letting her tell him if and when she wanted?

As a rule Mercy didn't talk much about her work. Which was fine. Fitzgerald didn't talk much about his either, meaning the work he used to do and maybe would again. Without discussing it, he and Mercy had reached an agreement: They lived in the present with few backward glances and few demands on one another.

What held them together was the river.

Mercy had grown up in Ossning, had fished the Borchard from childhood, and the DNR job was the only one she ever wanted. When chances had come to move up in the department's bureaucracy, she turned them down. Ossning was where she wanted to stay. He first met her a few miles from town on the Borchard's mainstream, the two of them fishing a Hendrickson spinner fall one evening. He liked her looks and the way she filled out her neoprenes and later that evening, fishing over, he asked her to the Black Duck in Kinnich for a drink.

He learned she had been married to Verlyn Kelso and had one child, and learned as well that he had a weakness for attractive women his age who knew more about the Borchard than he did and were better fly casters than he was. He had never known one before.

After that first evening he saw Mercy every time he came up to the river from Detroit, and when he won the lottery and moved to the river he asked her to marry him. He explained that his marriage had been dead a long time and winning the lottery made a funeral possible. Mercy didn't think the remark in good taste, but she agreed to think about his proposal. A short while later she brought her things out from town to the rented A-frame at Walther Bridge and they set up housekeeping together.

That surprised him some, Mercy's quickness to move in with him.

If you knew the north woods, she explained when he eventually asked her about it, it wasn't so surprising. It was sparsely settled country and there weren't many available partners, with the result that you grabbed whoever came along or happened at the moment to be available. "Thanks a lot," Fitzgerald said, but Mercy said she was talking in general. She didn't mean him, exactly.

Then there were the long winters and you needed some indoor sport to go along with ice fishing, running snowmobiles, and cross-country skiing. "It was summer when you moved in," Fitzgerald pointed out, but Mercy said that in the north woods you were always planning for winter. Her final reason was that she liked Fitzgerald, which in the north woods wasn't strictly necessary for a relationship and probably revealed a fundamental weakness in her character.

"I get the picture," Fitzgerald said.

Mercy's son, Kit, was nineteen and on his own now. He had dropped out of Central Michigan at Mount Pleasant—temporarily, Mercy insisted—and was working for his father at Kelso's Kabin Kamp. During the winter he visited the A-frame for dinner on a few occasions, spending most of the time looking over Fitzgerald's fishing equipment and fly-tying materials and the books on the shelves. Fitzgerald's impression of him was that he looked like Verlyn but didn't act like him. He barely opened his mouth. Mercy thought Kit was going through a phase. She said the only person he talked to was Calvin McCann.

When they reached the house yesterday Fitzgerald had made Mercy a hot whiskey and she took it into the bedroom. When he went in to check on her later she was asleep, the drink half finished. He turned off the light and took his own drink into the other bedroom, the one he had set up as an office for working on his novel, and settled down to read some Thoreau.

It was hard to concentrate given that he had Link Pickett's death in the back of his mind, and you had to concentrate to read Thoreau. *Walden* had been assigned reading in college but he never managed to finish the whole thing. He liked parts of the book but there were long airy passages where he stumbled, never able to fasten on anything solid. Something was there all right, something that caught his attention, but he wished Thoreau had kept to the facts and revealed more about himself and hadn't tried so hard to strike an impression.

Thoreau was twenty-eight when he went to the pond, and Fitzgerald—nearly two decades older—had decided it was really a book for the young, if the young could sit still long enough to read it. He finally found a key in an essay about Thoreau, the writer saying about *Walden* that it "steadfastly refuses to record bad news." When he read that, Fitzgerald realized it was Thoreau's optimism, his refusal to be grim, that he liked most about the book. *We think that we can change our clothes only,* Thoreau wrote at the end of a book whose whole point is the opposite. You probably had to be young to be stirred by that line, but Fitzgerald had decided it had some application to him, too.

A marriage behind him, maybe a career as well, it was a time for optimism. At his age you needed to read Thoreau with a few grains of salt and not get completely carried away or, the opposite, spin your wheels picking out holes in his thinking. You had to read him with a touch of adult cynicism. But Thoreau was on the right track, facing into life rather than away, and Fitzgerald was trying to follow. Thoreau had built a cabin on a pond; he had rented an A-frame on the Borchard. *There is more day to dawn,* Thoreau said, and Fitzgerald wholeheartedly agreed even though he was still pondering what the line actually meant.

Three drinks later, about two-thirty, he called it a night. In the bedroom, checking on Mercy, he pulled a down quilt up around her shoulders and decided to sleep on the single bed in his office. She needed an undisturbed night's rest.

But in bed Fitzgerald was wide awake and thinking of Link Pickett. He seemed all right the few times they met in town, a burly man with a weathered outdoor face with a stubble of beard on it. Yet it was hard to think of him apart from Verlyn Kelso's view that the canoe livery was responsible for every bad thing that happened on the Borchard.

Verlyn's self-interest was apparent, since the future of Kelso's Kabin Kamp depended on fishermen coming to the river, yet he wasn't alone in his condemnation of Link Pickett. Mercy had to be more circumspect, given her job. That was why, she explained to Fitzgerald once, she hadn't used Verlyn's name when they were married. She had to keep as much distance as possible from the Kabin Kamp. All the same, she didn't have many good things to say about canoes on the river. Neither did Nils or guides like Calvin McCann.

But to have your head taken off by a wire stretched across the river…that was a rough fate for anyone.

Fitzgerald found himself imagining what had happened at Danish Landing, forgetting Thoreau and staring into the black hole of bleak night.

SIX

"I HAVE TO TALK," Mercy said when he called her.

"Hotel?"

"Anywhere but. Everybody treats me like I'm going to come apart. Someplace anonymous."

"You say."

"Burger King."

After he hung up the phone Fitzgerald filled his mug again and went out on the deck for another look at the river. Sunlight was edging toward it. In mid-afternoon, sun full on the water, he might baptize the new season and try some fishing. Between Walther Bridge and Flint Road the mainstream of the Borchard was catch-and-release water, flies only, open all year. In early spring rainbows came up from deep water below Mentone to spawn on good gravel beneath slick water. Since St. Patrick's Day he had been on the lookout for beds and thought he might have spotted a few.

Before, living in Detroit, he used to drive to the Borchard this time of year, late March or early April, feeling the fishing itch after the eternal winter of the city. Always it was too early, the water still too cold, no rainbows in sight, spitting snow in the air and the rod guides freezing shut with ice, and he had a wonderful time for a couple of days. Always he went back to the city refreshed and full of energy.

Below him the river swung right in a long slow bend. The water was deep here and held big trout you didn't have a chance for unless a heavy hatch brought them up or you happened to drift a nymph just right and felt one hit, solid as if it had smashed a streamer. You braced yourself then for the pure joy of handling a big fish on a fine tippet.

Fitzgerald stayed on the deck, watching the sunlight advance toward the black water along the bend, until he finished his coffee. He went inside then and got ready. In the basement he found a picnic hamper and took a bottle of Valpolicella from a case he had bought in Traverse City. It was the red wine Colonel Cantwell drank in Hemingway's *Across the River and Into the Trees,* a disappointing book. But Fitzgerald had liked the duck hunting parts and the description of the black-painted gondolas and the open market across the Rialto Bridge, and he had learned to like the Colonel's wine. In town he would get things to go with it, fresh bread at the Six-Grain Bakery and sardines and cheese at the IGA.

The lunch might lift Mercy's spirits, if that was the problem.

THE DNR SUBURBAN was parked outside Burger King when he arrived, Mercy in it. He motioned her over to the Cherokee, told her to forget fast food, they were having a picnic lunch, and drove to the Ossning city park where in summer the East Branch of the Borchard flowed with the tranquility of an English chalk stream. Now, swollen with snow melt, it ran dark and fast with an undeniable look of a north woods spring.

Fitzgerald parked beside the water and uncorked the wine with a Swiss army knife he kept in the glove compartment for the purpose. "I'm working," Mercy said, but she took the plastic glass when he passed it to her. He set out the food, some on the dashboard and the rest on the padded console between the seats, and said, "The least I could do, sleeping through breakfast."

"You know," Mercy said, "at times you're sweet."

"Marry me then," Fitzgerald said.

"Give me another reason."

"I've got a few bucks."

"That's the trouble with you. You're not sweet for long."

"So we'll live off your money."

"Shut up," Mercy said, "and eat."

They ate slowly and licked their fingers because he had forgotten napkins and Mercy let him refill her glass with Valpolicella and didn't mention she was working.

"Can we talk now?" he asked when they were done and both holding glasses and leaning back against the doors.

"I saw Stroud this morning," Mercy said

"And?"

"He'd already talked with Rawlings again. We went over the same ground. Stroud keeps saying we messed up evidence by taking down the wire."

"The wire itself could be a help. He could find where it came from, that sort of thing."

"Maybe."

Fitzgerald said, "Something else on your mind?"

Mercy waited, looking at him, before she said, "I want you to help with this."

"Help how?"

"Investigate, I suppose. Look into what happened."

"We know what happened."

"Find out who did it, I meant. I know, everything points to Verlyn. Everyone just assumes he did it. He was my first thought, too. But there's more to it."

"Meaning it's too obvious, Verlyn doing it?"

"No."

"What then?"

"Just look into it, will you? Do some checking around. You know how to do that. You're a writer."

"I worked for a newspaper," Fitzgerald said. "Close, but not the same."

"Close enough."

Fitzgerald sipped his wine and looked at her. Mercy's hair was long and gray-blond, a disordered mass that he found appealing. She wore no makeup and didn't need any, her skin a light brown that would deepen to bronze with the summer. Her green DNR jacket was unzipped and beneath it a crisp tan shirt was open at the neck, revealing flawless skin and the thin gold necklace he had given her at Christmas.

"Let's go home," Fitzgerald said. "Take the afternoon off. We missed last night."

"Lord, I was tired."

"We'll make up for it."

"This afternoon," Mercy said, "I've got the report for Rawlings."

"You want to tell me what happened at Danish Landing?"

"Not really."

But then she did. She went over the details carefully, seemingly as much for herself as for him.

"We were waiting in cover when the canoe came around the bend with Link Pickett in it. We only saw the wire for the first time when the sun hit it. Then Rawlings and I both jumped up and started shouting at Link, trying to stop him, but he only straightened up in the canoe. He looked like he was about to lift his baseball cap.

"His body spun backward when he hit the wire, the canoe shooting ahead, and then his head seemed to dangle on his shoulder for a second; then he tipped sideways into the water. When Rawlings and I got down there we didn't need to do CPR or anything. There wasn't anything we could do.

"We managed to get Link partway up the bank. I'll never forget the look on his face—total surprise.

I don't know, maybe he died in an instant, before he even knew he was hurt.

"Rawlings told me to stay with the body while he followed the wire into the woods, get it unhooked. Then he went up to the Suburban and used the car phone to call for an ambulance. What he told Stroud, that unfastening the wire was instinctive, was the plain truth. We didn't discuss it. It just seemed important to get the wire down before anything else happened. Anyway, while Rawlings was up waiting by the Suburban for the ambulance, I stayed with Link's body on the bank."

"That was rough," Fitzgerald said.

Mercy stiffened and looked back at him, blue eyes suddenly fierce. "I've seen worse."

Fitzgerald doubted that but it wasn't a point to argue. There was something else he wanted to clarify. "Link raising up in the canoe, starting to lift his cap. What do you make of that?"

"I don't know."

"As a guess I'd say he knew you and Rawlings were there. He knew about the big sting operation."

"It was Rawlings' dumb idea," Mercy said.

"Sure it was. I know that. But Link may have been tipped off. After he lifted his cap he probably meant to give you the finger. Then he planned to slide past and never touch the sweeper. He'd have put one over on you and Rawlings."

"Maybe," Mercy said.

"Anybody know about the sting other than you and Rawlings?"

"I don't know."

Fitzgerald waited a moment before he said, "You don't seem very interested."

"Of course I am. That's why I want you checking around."

Fitzgerald waited again, looking at her, trying to read something in her eyes. He sipped more of his wine, finished it, and said, "Let's take a walk." The sun was straight overhead now, full on the water. "I want a closer look, see if any bugs have the courage to consider hatching."

"The water's too cold and will be for another month," she said, but finished her wine and got out the other side of the Cherokee.

They followed a path through the park that ran alongside the river. The tree cover, sugar maples and some planted spruce, was thin and most of the snow melted. The air felt even more like spring than it had on the mainstream of the Borchard. In the summer, the East Branch warm as a farm pond, kids from town caught big chubs in slow water.

When they came to a picnic table, the top matted with soggy leaves, Fitzgerald stopped and asked, "Why are you so concerned? Why not let the case rest with Stroud?"

"You know why."

"Tell me anyway."

She looked at him hard, blue eyes fierce again. "In case you've forgotten, Verlyn happens to be the father of my son. I'd rather he wasn't a murderer. That's why."

Fitzgerald took a deep breath and plunged in. "There's a possibility he is. You know it, Stroud knows it, everyone in Ossning knows it."

"Then see what else. You know, extenuating circumstances or something. I don't know."

"Verlyn needs a big-time lawyer," Fitzgerald said, "not me."

"Does that mean you won't help?"

He reached out and drew her to him. He smoothed hair from her face and kissed her until he felt her body lean into his, kissing him back. "Don't expect anything," he whispered.

"Thank you," she whispered back.

LATER, WALKING BACK TO the Cherokee, holding hands, she said, "There's one more thing. I didn't tell Stroud, but he probably knows anyway. Up here everybody knows everything. It's about Link's wife. Laurel Pickett and I, we went through school together. We're friends—not close, but friends."

"Is that important?"

"Just listen," Mercy said. "Okay?"

"Okay."

"When Rawlings came up with his hair-brained plan to trap Link clearing sweepers—well, I did something. Something, technically speaking, I shouldn't have."

"Go on."

"You have to understand Ossning and Link's place in town. You have to understand the whole north woods, as a matter of fact. The way things work up here. If the DNR had prosecuted Link it would have thrown everything out of balance. Protecting the river—protecting the environment—it takes a lot of good will from a lot of people who tend to dislike the DNR on principle. I mean there are things up here that can't be legislated and I've worked hard to get them. Important things. If Link were prosecuted we'd have to start from scratch.''

''And Rawlings doesn't understand that?''

''He doesn't have a clue about working with real people leading real lives. He believes all you need are laws and a big stick.''

''I think I get it,'' Fitzgerald said.

''Do you?''

''What I think you're saying is you told Laurel Pickett about the sting.''

Mercy said, ''Damned right I did.''

SEVEN

THEN MERCY came apart.

She clung to him, sobbing, hard body trembling. Fitzgerald wrapped his arms around her and said nothing. There wasn't anything to say until she got the tears out of her system. The guilt she was feeling would take longer to shed.

When she drew away she wiped her eyes, blew her nose, and apologized. "That was embarrassing."

"Forget it."

"I never cry, Fitzgerald."

"I know you don't."

"It's just—"

"I'd have done the same thing. You know the community and Rawlings doesn't."

"That's not what I mean," Mercy said, and rubbed her eyes again. "I told Laurel to tell Link and she must have. He was ready for us out there. You could tell he wasn't going to cut the sweeper, riding the canoe down the middle of the stream that way. When he heard us yelling at him he must have become confused. The plan was to hold our cover until he started cutting. He knew that. When we saw the wire and started yelling he raised up—you know, as if he was startled—and it was just enough for the wire to catch him.''

"Otherwise he would have gone under."

"Yes."

"But you had to try to warn him," Fitzgerald said. "You saw the wire and you yelled. What else could you have done?"

"You still don't get it. It's not that. It's that Laurel must have told someone other than Link—someone who then strung the wire at Danish Landing. That's where I screwed up. I'm responsible."

Fitzgerald said, "Laurel is if she told someone else."

"But I told *her.*"

THEY LEFT IT that way and Fitzgerald drove her back to Burger King. Mercy said she wanted to use the restroom to dab her eyes with water before she went back to work. Fitzgerald drove toward town then and turned off on the South Downriver Road and went past Pickett's Canoe Livery.

It was a big black-log building with a lawn that swept down to the river's edge and a launching deck. In summer the lawn was kept as manicured as a golf green and there were planter boxes of petunias spaced along the river. It was one of the things that irritated Verlyn, the postcard-pretty look of the place on a river that was supposed to be covered by the Wild and Scenic Rivers Act. Each year he complained to Mercy, and each year she had to tell him the Borchard was classified as "scenic'' under the act rather than ''wild.'' Besides, the act didn't cover the domesticated stretch of the mainstream on the edge of town where the canoe livery was located.

The livery still had the melancholy look of a summer business in winter. Rows of aluminum canoes were stacked on the lawn and the vertical carriers that returned them from take-out sites lined the parking area. Along with renting canoes, the livery supplied provisions and camping equipment for the three-night trip to the first dam that interrupted the flow of the river toward Lake Huron. This side of the business appeared dormant as well. Two Chevy pickup trucks parked on the gravel drive that led to the entrance were the only signs of life. One was Link Pickett's, two-tone blue, with the livery name painted on the door. The other, a metallic gray with a canoe resting in the bed, was one Fitzgerald had noticed Brand Pickett driving around town.

He pulled in the drive, stopped behind the trucks, and walked up to the entrance. There was a buzzer at the door but it was apparently disconnected. When he tried it no sound came from inside. He knocked and when there was no answer he banged hard on the door. He heard shuffling inside, then distinct footsteps, before Brand Pickett swung the door open.

''Sorry about the racket,'' Fitzgerald said.

Brand was a younger version of his brother— beefy linebacker shoulders, dark beard that looked like it was shaved every third or fourth day, eyes too small for his face and set too far apart. The eyes made him look like he was squinting at something he couldn't quite make out. He even dressed the way Link did—blue jeans, wide leather belt with a silver buckle, wool shirts in winter and sleeveless T-shirts in summer. Today he had a down vest over a wool shirt and from the look on his face, irritated, he had been interrupted at something. He didn't move from the doorway.

"My name's Fitzgerald. Link and I talked a few times in town. I was just driving by, saw the trucks, and thought I'd stop and tell you how sorry I am about Link."

"You're the one hit the lottery," Brand said.

"Actually, I thought Link's wife might be here. She's a friend of Mercy Virdon and Mercy's a friend of mine."

"Friend?" Brand sniffed. "You live together."

"She isn't here?"

Brand didn't answer. His narrowed eyes seemed to be looking through Fitzgerald at something in the distance.

"Anyway," Fitzgerald said, "tell her I stopped." Then he said, "It's lousy about Link. If there's anything I can do—" Brand's eyes suddenly blinked shut. When they opened again Fitzgerald felt a momentary rush of sympathy for the man.

"You want to do something?"

"Name it."

"Tell your friend Verlyn not to turn his back."

Fitzgerald tried a thin smile before he said, "We're not exactly friends."

"Tell him something else. I'm changing the name of the fly shop. No more Tackle Box. It's going to be Discount Tackle and I'll undercut everything he sells at his place."

"As I said, we're not all that close."

"He doesn't like canoes?" Brand barged on. "Tell him I'm renting jet skis next. You know those things? They're going to roar past the lodge like freight trains. He can figure on plenty of empty rooms."

"I don't think jet skis are legal on the river."

"Legal? What's legal got to do with it? Killing Link wasn't legal but he's dead anyway."

"I take your point."

"Verlyn won't be hearing anyway," Brand said, an edge of disappointment in his voice while his pin-point eyes glittered with pleasure. "Not from no prison cell."

"You might," Fitzgerald offered, "be jumping to conclusions."

Brand ignored him. "Better yet," he said before shutting the door, "from no coffin."

FITZGERALD HAD nothing in mind when he stopped at the canoe livery. It seemed a way of beginning, of getting his feet wet and seeing what might turn up. Newspaper work was the same. You poked around in a story, working blind, and if you were lucky you turned up something to write about. Real lucky, you turned up something good to write about. If looking into Link Pickett's murder wasn't the same as newspaper work, then Fitzgerald had no idea how to proceed.

Brand Pickett's response was about what he expected. Except for one thing: There had been a staged quality to it, an excess, like an actor projecting too hard to reach the rear seats. That Brand had settled on Verlyn as Link's killer was no surprise. Most of Ossning had probably reached the same conclusion by now. What struck a wrong note was Link pouring it out to a virtual stranger.

On the other hand, maybe he said the same thing to everyone and hoped it would get back to Willard Stroud, keeping the heat on the sheriff to nail Verlyn. Brand couldn't have thought Fitzgerald would carry a message back to Verlyn. He could call up Verlyn and do that himself. Mercy had told him that Link and Verlyn regularly used the phone to berate each other for misdeeds. When they ran into each other in Ossning or on the Borchard they fell into a stony silence.

Fitzgerald drove into town and turned onto the main drag toward the community hospital. There was a planted grove of Norway spruce and white birch on a side street just to the north, with a winding asphalt road through it leading to Link Pickett's house. Fitzgerald slowed down and could see a half-dozen cars parked on the road and caught a glimpse of the house, a modern brick ranch-style affair. Verlyn probably didn't care for the look of Link's house, either.

He swung back on the main drag and passed the hotel, heading for the parking lot of the city-county building. Inside he gave his name to the sheriff's secretary, a tiny blue-haired woman in a pink sweatshirt with glittering appliqué on the front who Fitzgerald was pretty sure was Willard Stroud's wife. Nepotism was never an issue in the north woods. Jobs were few and it was assumed that family and friends would be taken care of before strangers.

"I'm not working," Fitzgerald announced when the secretary sent him into Stroud's office. "You'd know otherwise."

Stroud looked him over carefully, peering across a plain wooden desk devoid of papers. The room was compact, orderly, and had diplomas on the side walls from law-enforcement seminars Stroud had attended in Lansing. Against the wall across from the desk was a bank of filing cabinets and above them a large framed map of Tamarack County.

"What that means," Fitzgerald went on, "is I'm not writing anything. That kind of work." When Stroud kept looking at him Fitzgerald added, "I don't want any confusion."

"Then maybe you'd better explain."

Fitzgerald nodded. He had a natural tendency to think the best of fly fishermen, and Stroud was a fly fisherman. But there was more to the man than that. He had a shrewd face and within was a watchful mind and maybe a good one, too. He didn't want to stir up any unnecessary trouble with Stroud.

"Mercy asked me to look around a little. Nothing special. Just see if I can find out anything, be of help."

Stroud idly lifted a hand to his shirt pocket, discovered it empty, lowered the hand back to the desk. "You ever smoke?" he asked.

"Didn't everyone?"

"Mercy got the idea I can't handle the case?"

Fitzgerald shook his head. "Nothing like that."

"Just a woman thing?"

"More or less."

"You're a citizen," Stroud said. "Do what you want. You know enough to keep out of the way."

"Right."

"You run across anything, you let me know."

"Agreed."

Stroud waited a minute, still examining Fitzgerald, before he said, "You got a bright idea where to look?"

Fitzgerald decided to put the cards Mercy had given him on the table. Some of them. "The wire at Danish Landing was exactly where Mercy and Rawlings had set up the sting operation to trap Link. That seems odd."

"Odd things happen."

"Or somebody was tipped off. He knew Link would be on the river, and he knew where Link'd be cutting a sweeper. This time of year that's fast water coming around the bend. The canoe would have some steam up. And there's another thing: Stringing the wire where Mercy and Rawlings would be suggests that whoever did it wanted witnesses. It could have been strung elsewhere, below other stretches of fast water. Having it at Danish Landing meant Mercy and Rawlings would see the whole thing.''

"I thought of that," Stroud said. "But whoever did it, he might have been in the dark. He might not have known about the DNR stunt. He just knew Link was on the river, cutting sweepers, and the one at Danish Landing was the next one to get."

Fitzgerald said, "Maybe. But it's odd."

Stroud shrugged. "Why would whoever did it want witnesses?"

"I don't know. Maybe he's the kind of ghoul who needs that. He gets pleasure hearing it talked about. Or maybe he didn't mean to kill Link. He meant to do some damage, and Mercy and Rawlings would be there to help. They'd get Link out of the river and into town. Maybe what happened is the whole business got out of hand."

"Way out." Stroud waited then, silent, thinking or whatever he was doing behind a shrewd face, before he said, "Let me tell you a story."

"Sure," Fitzgerald said.

"Some kids on snowmobiles were raising hell along the river three or four winters ago. They paid no attention to no-trespassing signs or young pines or any sensitive undergrowth and there was drinking involved and a trail of beer cans. There were also some break-ins at closed-up cabins and parties that went on for days and carpets urinated on and graffiti left scrawled on walls.

"I couldn't get a handle on it right away so some of the people out there, permanent residents on the river, decided to take matters in their own hands. Verlyn Kelso was the ringleader, whipping everybody up, telling them they had to protect their property. You know what he did on his own place?"

"I think you're going to tell me," Fitzgerald said.

"He strung wire about three feet off the ground with no warnings of any sort—no signs, no colored cloth tied to the wire, nothing. So I went out and had a conversation with him and told him to take the wire down. Verlyn couldn't understand why. I told him if some kid on a snowmobile came roaring through the woods and hit that wire and killed himself then he would damned well understand why."

Stroud paused. "You see what I'm getting at?"

"I believe so," Fitzgerald said.

"That's not the half of it. I could tell you a dozen stories and they'd all point in the same direction. There's the time Verlyn set up a bow-and-arrow range across the river from the Kabin Kamp and waited 'til canoeists were coming down to begin practicing. Or the time he went into Canoe Rest at night and used an ice pick on canoes of a touring club from Grand Rapids. I won't mention the times he's put on waders and gone in the river and overturned a canoe because people were making too much noise coming downstream. You got any idea how often I've had to deal with him?''

"Probably not."

"One time he overturned a whole Girl Scout troop. After that he went after some Seventh Day Adventists from Andrews University."

Fitzgerald said, "You've talked with Verlyn about Link's death?"

Stroud hesitated. "Maybe I have."

Fitzgerald said quickly, "I shouldn't have asked. My mistake."

"That's so."

Fitzgerald got up to leave. He didn't want Stroud getting his back up before there was any reason. There could be soon enough. "I wonder if you'd tell me one thing," he said from the doorway. "Link must have made plans that morning to be met downriver. Or else he spotted a vehicle to bring the canoe back to the livery."

"There were plans."

"His brother was meeting him?"

"Link and Brand spotted Link's truck at Foegelman Road."

"And Link never made it. So, afterward, Brand picked up the canoe himself. It's still in his truck."

"We released it to him," Stroud said.

"Sure," Fitzgerald said. Then he changed the subject. "I'm thinking of wetting a line this afternoon. See if any rainbows have come up yet. You think I'm pushing things a little?"

"Probably."

"I get spring fever."

"So do I," Stroud said. "Then something happens and I've got a job to do."

BEFORE HE DROVE BACK downriver Fitzgerald wanted a cup of coffee. He also wanted to gauge how the wind was blowing in Ossning. He stopped in front of the Six-Grain Bakery on the main drag and went inside.

The bakery, with a few tables grouped along a wall, was a town meeting place during the winter when people wanted a quick escape from the monotonous green and white of the landscape and were willing to strike up a conversation with whoever was sitting beside them. Fitzgerald had stopped often as a way of getting acquainted. Now, the middle of the afternoon and spring in the air, he was the only customer. Bonnie Pym, the woman who worked the bakery counter, brought him a mug of freshly-made coffee and reminded him he hadn't stopped to talk with her in a while.

"You avoiding me, sugar?"

Fitzgerald said, "You know better than that, Bonnie," and gave her his best smile.

"You see the story in the Detroit paper," Bonnie asked him, "the one about Link getting killed? Everybody in town's talking about it. We won't get Gus Thayer's story in the *Call* 'til Thursday, a weekly an' all." She brought Fitzgerald a wrinkled copy of the *Free Press* from behind the counter and flipped to an inside page.

It was an Associated Press story, two inches with a single-column head, that emphasized the manner of Link Pickett's death and the fact that he was a prominent Ossning businessman. The final line quoted the Tamarack County sheriff, Willard Stroud, as saying the murder was under investigation.

"I don't know what for," Bonnie Pym said.

She was a trim brunette about Fitzgerald's age who wore long earrings and short skirts. She was just shy of being pretty. Before he met Mercy, Fitzgerald had been interested enough to inquire whether or not she was married. She wasn't, but had been, and he realized he knew all three of her ex-husbands. They were all fly fishermen he had met on the river or hanging around Verlyn's shop or the Black Duck in Kinnich. Without having to think about it very much Fitzgerald decided to keep his distance.

"Open and shut, huh?" he asked her.

"You don't think so?"

He shrugged and waited for Bonnie to relate the Ossning consensus.

"I mean, Verlyn hated Link's guts. Everybody knows that."

"That's the problem."

When Bonnie frowned at him, puzzled, he let her go on with the usual list of grievances Verlyn had with Link. He didn't bother to tell her that everyone who loved the river for fishing had the same list.

"Laurel's in seclusion, but she talked with

friends on the phone and accused Verlyn of the murder. And some people who came in here today saw Brand and he said the sheriff had to the end of the week to arrest Verlyn for the murder. After that Brand would take care of Verlyn himself. You can't blame him," Bonnie said.

"I suppose not."

"Brand can be mean."

"So I've heard."

"Hey, sugar," Bonnie said, and rolled her eyes, "I *know* he can."

When Fitzgerald finished his coffee he said, "Thanks for pointing out the story in the paper. I might not have seen it otherwise."

Bonnie winked at him. "Anything for a customer." Then she asked, "Mind writing down some numbers?"

"It's a waste of time, Bonnie."

"Ain't everything, sugar?"

RATHER THAN make the drive down to the cabin on the South Branch, Fitzgerald played a hunch and took the South Downriver Road, the asphalt road paralleling the Borchard's mainstream, and finally angling down to the water at Walther Bridge. There was a pickup parked in the crushed-stone lot at Kelso's Kabin Kamp alongside Verlyn's big Land Rover, though the lodge and the fly shop wouldn't officially open for business until a week before opening day of the fishing season. Verlyn always started up on opening day and then closed for winter just after the bow-and-arrow season for deer.

Mercy had told Fitzgerald the story of the place.

Verlyn's grandfather had bought land along the Borchard before there was a road down to the water and a bridge across, thinking of it as a private fishing camp where he could hike in and pitch a tent in summer and haul out the grayling that jammed the river. After the road and bridge were built, Verlyn's father started the commercial operation. It had been just some rough log cabins scattered through the woods and a café run by his mother, the place frequented only by fishermen who walked around all day in waders.

His father and mother had given the place its name, and after they were gone Verlyn had taken over. He remodeled everything, replacing the old cabins with a peeled-log lodge and a new dining room with a bar and enlarging the fly shop and adding a line of archery equipment and finally building a log place for himself set back in the woods. Mercy had urged him to change the name of the business to something more befitting the new class of clientele it attracted. Some of the people who stayed at the Kabin Kamp barely wet a line. They hung around the fly shop talking with Verlyn and sat out in front of the lodge on wooden patio furniture drinking cocktails and watching the river. For a new name Mercy favored something simple and classy like The Lodge on the Borchard, pointing out that the initials of Kelso's Kabin Kamp, if anyone thought about them, had an unfortunate connotation.

Verlyn said that was what he liked about the name.

Fitzgerald drove past and stopped on the bridge. There was a view downriver for a hundred yards or so before the river bent to the right, beginning the deep hole beneath his A-frame. The day was still bright and cloudless, and when he rolled down the window he gauged the temperature at about fifty, probably a half-dozen degrees or so warmer than the river. A lone fisherman was moving slowly downstream and from the look of his casts he was bouncing a weighted egg fly along the bottom. Every now and then he paused and glanced up at the sky as if he couldn't believe his good fortune, a spring day in Michigan in April. He wore a big Western stetson with a curled brim and you could see a gray ponytail dangling beneath.

Fitzgerald left the window open and thumped down on the accelerator, his stomach suddenly tight with anticipation. He should have rigged a rod before he left. Now, doing it quickly, he might bungle everything, tie a bad knot that would give way when a fat rainbow came off a bed and smacked the fly.

"Take it easy," he told himself. "You've got the whole season."

In another voice he answered, "And you've got other things on your mind."

EIGHT

CALVIN HAD FISHED through the run and was thinking of working his way back upriver to the Kabin Kamp and some hot coffee when he noticed the fisherman behind him, just at the head of the run, and recognized Fitzgerald's hat.

It was Irish, Fitzgerald had told him, and indestructible. From the look of it, a beat-up brown tweed, Calvin thought that was doubtful. But the main problem was the brim. It was too narrow and didn't give enough protection from the sun. He had advised Fitzgerald about the danger of skin cancer and suggested he get a hat like his own, one that shielded a man's face and had a wide band where he could stick a pheasant feather.

Fitzgerald tossed a hand in the air and Calvin signaled back. Then he crossed to the opposite bank and got out of the water in a stand of bare alders and white birch and studied Fitzgerald as he fished the run. He was okay as far as casting went, though you could tell he was rusty from the winter and impatient at the same time. He was too short with the back cast, rushing things. But Calvin gave him credit otherwise.

Fitzgerald was from Detroit and made a living working for a scandal sheet down there before he won the lottery and came up to the Borchard and rented a plush house and settled in for a year, living off the fat of the land. That added up to a lot against him in Calvin's book. Plenty of rich city types were into fly fishing and showed up on the river and Calvin took their money as a guide and ignored them otherwise. And he didn't believe in lotteries. He had read up on them. What they amounted to was a tax on the poor.

Yet as far as Calvin could tell the money hadn't changed Fitzgerald, except for the way he was living now and the new vehicle he drove. He had met him before, when Fitzgerald came up to the Borchard on short trips and hung around Verlyn's shop, picking up information about hatches and hot spots. He and Fitzgerald had struck up some conversations about books.

Fitzgerald still hung around the shop and now and then he told Calvin about a book he ought to read, and Mercy Virdon had moved in with him, which was a good sign. Calvin considered Mercy a woman of good taste. For a while after she left Verlyn she had gone around with him, and something might have come of it except that Mercy had a job that ruled out spending half the year in New Zealand.

"Anything?" Calvin called out after Fitzgerald had fished through the run and was working his way against the current to the other side of the stream.

"Didn't expect anything," Fitzgerald called back.

He waited until Fitzgerald came up to him. Then he said, "I took the water temperature when I got in."

"And?"

"Forty-six. At fifty the rainbows might begin moving. Until then, casting, we're just getting exercise."

"I saw some beds that looked fresh."

"Maybe," Calvin said. "It's hard to tell. Water temperature's the best indicator."

Fitzgerald came out of the stream and stood beside him in the stand of birch, water draining from his waders. He leaned his rod against a tree. "You could use some new equipment," Calvin said. "You look a little tacky out there."

"Thanks a lot."

"I've got some good blanks. You could wrap a new rod."

"I don't know," Fitzgerald said. "I get used to something I hate to lose the feel. You know what I mean?" Then he said, "Heard you were back, Calvin. Day like this I figured you'd be out."

"Spring fever."

"Like hell," Fitzgerald said, and grinned at him under the Irish tweed hat. "You just left fall. How can you have spring fever when you missed winter?"

"A figure of speech," Calvin said.

"How was it down there?"

"Big browns, good women, food without poison in it."

"Sounds like heaven."

"Except the economy's more screwed up than ours. EEC farm tariffs, they're killing the country. I got a book about it."

"We'll get together." Then Fitzgerald said, "You going back to Verlyn's now?"

"I'm giving it some thought."

"Verlyn working?"

"He's getting the inventory straightened around," Calvin said, "and fussing with the guide schedule. I was helping him with that. It was more fooling around than work."

"You know what happened?" Fitzgerald asked him.

"Who doesn't."

"Verlyn say anything about it?"

"You know Verlyn," Calvin said.

"What did he say?"

"The world's a better place with that sonofabitch Link Pickett out of it."

"Jesus," Fitzgerald said.

"Willard Stroud hasn't been out yet. I asked Verlyn and he acted like he didn't know what I was talking about. Why Stroud would want to see him."

"Stroud's probably letting him dangle a while."

"Hell," Calvin said, "that won't bother Verlyn."

"You're probably right." Fitzgerald retrieved his rod and turned back to the river. Over his shoulder he said, "Stop by my place before you go to Verlyn's. Something I want to ask you."

CALVIN LOOKED THROUGH the books while Fitzgerald was in the kitchen. He had taken off his waders and, waist down, was in polypropylene long johns and thick wool socks, the same as Fitzgerald. Most of the books were novels checked out of the Ossning public library, the kind of books Calvin didn't read. He had never gotten the hang of novels. He heard enough make-believe stories from fishermen to need any more. Fitzgerald was supposed to be writing a novel himself, so maybe the library books were models, showing him how to do it.

Fitzgerald came out of the kitchen with two glasses and a plastic container of orange juice. "The real thing, no concentrate." He showed Calvin the container so he could read the fine-print information on the label.

"I'll take your word for it," Calvin said, and Fitzgerald poured both glasses to the top.

They sat in front of the stone fireplace, their feet up on a coffee table that was rough-cut from a copper beech and heaped with books, sunlight streaming in the room from the wall of glass behind them.

Calvin asked, "How'd the winter go?"

"Not bad as far as cold, but plenty of snow and some ice storms that took out the electricity for long stretches. We lived with propane lanterns and wood fires."

"Any cross-country?"

"Some," Fitzgerald said. "I actually lost a few pounds over the winter. Usually I pick up some."

"You can't beat cross-country for the ticker," Calvin said.

"You don't miss skiing in New Zealand?"

Calvin thought about that before he said, "Not enough. You tie much during the winter?"

"Not as much as I figured, around the house all the time. But I learned some things, thanks to Mercy. I'm a little better."

"Mercy's good," Calvin said. "I taught her."

"She gives Verlyn some credit, too."

"That's fair," Calvin admitted.

"Speaking of whom," Fitzgerald said.

Fitzgerald sipped his orange juice and looked straight ahead at the fireplace, thinking, Calvin waiting for him, in no hurry. He wondered if Fitzgerald knew what he had going with Laurel Pickett, Link's widow now. He might. Laurel and Mercy knew each other from school and women liked to talk, though he wasn't sure if women talked about things like that. So Fitzgerald might know. If he did, and if Mercy did, it might have crossed their minds what had crossed Laurel's, that he was the one who had gotten rid of Link. On the face of it, Calvin realized, he had a motive.

Fitzgerald said finally, "Mercy asked me to do some checking around about Link."

"You were a cop before you worked on the scandal sheet?"

Fitzgerald ignored him. "Everyone assumes Verlyn's the killer, but Mercy doesn't believe it, or doesn't want to. She thinks it's too obvious."

"She's right."

"You're positive?"

Calvin said, "You know Verlyn. In his cups he'd say there was a bounty out on Link and he was going to claim it. He'd tell anyone. I heard it a hundred times."

"That's Mercy's point. You don't talk like that, then do it."

"On the other hand, we're talking about Verlyn. He could be sly enough to shoot off his mouth and go ahead anyway. Or dumb enough. Take your pick."

"When he's worked up," Fitzgerald said, "he always says he's going to kill someone."

"Not as much as he said it about Link."

"So you think it's possible he did it?"

"What I think," Calvin said, "is Stroud's got himself a time proving it."

Fitzgerald stared at the fireplace again, thinking again, and Calvin waited him out. Mounted across the front of the fireplace about halfway up the stone was a big Atlantic sailfish that the owner, a business tycoon from Detroit who Calvin had heard about from Verlyn but never met, had probably caught in the Florida Keys and brought up for his Michigan place. Calvin considered it tacky to mount any fish, especially one from out of state and salt water, and he thought about mentioning it to Fitzgerald. Fitzgerald ought to take it down while he was renting the place. It wasn't right having to glance up while you were at your bench tying tricos in size twenty-two and see a monster foreign fish like that.

Fitzgerald said, "There's another thing, Calvin. It's about Kit."

"The kid?"

"As far as I know, Mercy hasn't put two and two together yet. Maybe Stroud hasn't either. But he will."

"Hold on," Calvin said. "What are we talking about?"

"Over the winter Kit moved out of the Kabin Kamp and took up living in a tent on the river. Roughing it. When Mercy found out she went flying off to Verlyn and they had a battle royal. I didn't hear about it from her."

"Who?"

"Jan told me. Mercy said to get Kit back home or she would and Verlyn said to hell with it, the kid needed to grow up, and spending some winter in a tent might help. Apparently, Verlyn had been giving Kit a hard time. Riding him. You know Verlyn. So the kid took off to show the old man what he could do. Mercy was upset, of course, and went out to see Kit and found at least he had good equipment. Arctic sleeping bag, propane heater, plenty of fire wood, that sort of thing. I stayed out of it because Mercy told me to. We had Kit over to the house for dinner a few times and he seemed all right, healthy enough and eating enough, and Mercy felt a little better about it. You could see it was a thing between Verlyn and Kit, each trying to out-macho the other.''

Calvin said, "We did that as kids. Verlyn and me, we lived on the South Branch a whole year. The only way we could get to town in winter was on skis.''

"Kit has that old Toyota, at least.''

"It'll be good for the kid.''

"Maybe. But that's not the point.''

"What is then?''

"Where Kit's pitched his tent. Jan told me. He's in the campground at Danish Landing. The road's kept plowed down to the river. He can hike into the campground from the road.''

"They got pit toilets there. On the South Branch we had the woods.''

"C'mon, Calvin,'' Fitzgerald said. "Kit's living near where Link Pickett was killed.''

"Meaning what?''

"That he could have seen who strung the wire. Or worse.''

"Hold on,'' Calvin said. "You thinking the kid could have done it?''

"I'm asking what you think,'' Fitzgerald said. "That's why we're sitting here drinking this organic orange juice.''

NINE

AT VERLYN'S. Back for dinner.

Fitzgerald was the only man Mercy had known who left scraps of paper around with accounts of his whereabouts. With Verlyn she was lucky to learn when he left town. One time he was at a fly fishing exposition in Chicago for a week before she realized he wasn't around anymore. She had picked up Fitzgerald's habit and left notes for him around the house.

As far as day-to-day communication went, their relationship couldn't be better, which probably stood to reason given that he worked for a newspaper, or had once. What she was uncertain about was what he was thinking, really thinking, when he was reading for long periods, a whiskey in his hand, eyes narrowed to the page. He seemed lost in deep thought then. On the other hand, she wasn't certain men thought at all but only acted on strange primeval impulses.

Tonight she didn't have a thought in her own head. She was glad to be away from work, away from town—away from Fitzgerald, for that matter. In the kitchen she made a whiskey and water, no ice—another thing she had picked up from Fitzgerald—and took it into the living room.

It was dark outside, the night made darker by the wall of pine beyond the glass-walled front of the room. She took the deep leather chair, the one Fitzgerald usually read in, and put up her feet on the coffee table. She didn't switch on the lamp. She wanted to sit here in the dark and drink and not think. She had been thinking all day and where had it gotten her?

Confused.

Worse than that, worried.

SHE CAME UP out of sleep when the back door opened and she heard voices in the kitchen, a man and a woman's, and recognized both of them. She switched on the light, swept hair back from her eyes, and was ready when Jan and Fitzgerald came down the hallway into the room. Fitzgerald had the whiskey bottle and glasses and Jan was carrying a pitcher of water.

"Jan needs a drink," Fitzgerald said, which Mercy could see for herself. Jan's hair was a mess, her eyes blotched from crying, her cheeks puffy. Mercy enjoyed the sight while she waited, expecting to hear the back door open again.

Jan must have read her mind. She said, "Verlyn isn't with us." Then tears welled up in her eyes again.

Fitzgerald got her settled in a chair and poured out a large drink. "It's a long story," he said. "Calvin and I came in afterward. Stroud had been at their place and he and Verlyn had a major dust up. Verlyn's still there. Jan will tell you.''

But Jan wasn't about to relate anything quickly. Once she got her tears under control she concentrated on her drink, holding it with both hands as if she thought Fitzgerald might snatch it back. Jan—even Jan like this, totally frazzled—made Mercy feel tall, awkward, tossed together, and overly-sexed. In her usual state Jan was a size six strawberry blond who looked as if she just had her hair done and who dressed, now that she presided over the lodge part of Kelso's Kabin Kamp, in a kind of permanent-press khaki safari outfit.

Whatever she wore she gave off a pale virginal glow even though, with Verlyn, she was on her second husband but with no children to show for it. You couldn't imagine Jan with children. Children meant sex and you couldn't imagine Jan shucking off the safari outfit or mussing her hair. She was a full-time helpmate. She was the kind of woman, Mercy imagined, that authors thanked in their books for unstinting devotion and selfless service while they spent years sealed away in their studies. Every time she read something like that in one of Fitzgerald's books Mercy felt like sending the woman a poison-pen letter.

After she and Verlyn called it quits he swung a hundred-and-eighty degrees. Now he had what he wanted, a wife who thought he was God's gift to humankind, who wouldn't say boo no matter how dumb he behaved, whose sole function in life was keeping him fed and clothed, all the while looking tiny and attractive and—damn it all—nearly perfect.

Mercy wasn't fooled. Jan was younger than Verlyn, so the odds were good she would outlive him. She would end up with the lodge and the fly shop, which whether she wanted to operate them or not were gold mines as property, making her a wealthy woman by Ossning standards. Beneath Jan's prim exterior, Mercy knew, another woman lurked.

Merry widow.

Rich bitch.

That Jan she understood—and preferred to the present one. She would be hovering around when the other Jan emerged—a pale evening dun, as Mercy imagined it, transformed into a swirling stone fly. Jan would have to realize that Kit, Verlyn's son and heir, had to be reckoned with. Kit was at least going to run the fly shop, if that was what he wanted to do, or he was going to share in the disposal of the entire property.

Mercy would see to that.

If Jan got in the way there would be more than a poison-pen letter.

"VERLYN'S SO STUBBORN," Jan said. "It makes things worse."

Mercy said, "You've noticed, huh?"

"Jan means with Stroud," Fitzgerald said. "When he showed up."

Mercy said, "I'm following. Jan speaks English."

Fitzgerald had freshened Jan's drink and was hovering around, solicitous the way men invariably were in her presence. They treated her like fragile crystal that was liable to break at any moment. Actually, she looked more like fine china now. With the first drink in her Jan had excused herself and gone to the bathroom, coming back with her hair combed and fresh lipstick on and her virginal glow mostly back in operation.

"The sheriff said the reason he stopped was to gather information. It was entirely routine. He wanted to know where Verlyn had been at the time of the accident. He was asking everyone who had a connection with Link Pickett. He was very polite."

"Accident?" Mercy interrupted.

But Jan went on, not missing a beat now that the tears had dried up and she was on a second drink, telling Mercy the story while looking mostly at Fitzgerald.

"Verlyn blew up. He said if the sheriff expected him to be sorry Link was dead he could forget it. In fact, during the funeral he was thinking of throwing a celebration party—an open house at the fly shop for all the fishermen on the river. The best thing to happen to them since the adoption of catch-and-release was Link's death. They ought to put a plaque on the river, commemorating it. Verlyn just went on and on that way. I couldn't do a thing with him. Then he told the sheriff he wasn't answering any questions and ordered him out of the shop.''

''Swell,'' Mercy said.

''The sheriff said that wasn't very smart on Verlyn's part. He could take him into town and question him there if he wanted to. The fact that Verlyn had already told some people in town he'd killed Link was all the grounds he needed.''

''Wait a minute,'' Mercy said. ''Verlyn actually *said* that?''

''Yes.''

''Good Lord.''

''But he never meant it,'' Jan said. ''You know how he talks.''

''Vaguely.''

''Well, do you know what Verlyn told the sheriff then?''

''Tell us.''

''Bullshit.''

Jan winced, having to use a word like that, and closed her eyes for a moment. Beside her Fitzgerald winced in sympathy.

''A favorite expression,'' Mercy said, ''I seem to recall.''

''Anyway,'' Jan said when she recovered, ''Verlyn and the sheriff went back and forth, shouting at one another. The sheriff kept saying he ought to take Verlyn in and Verlyn said he didn't have any evidence and if he did take him in he'd sue Tamarack County for every cent it had and ever would have. The sheriff would have to go back to earning a living like everyone else.''

''Verlyn has a gift for sweet talk,'' Mercy said.

''The sheriff got so mad I thought he might have a heart attack. But Verlyn wouldn't let up. He started talking about his lawyer and said if the sheriff came back he'd better plan to make an arrest. And if he did, Clappman would be there to check out everything. The county hadn't better make any mistakes because it was going to pay through the nose.''

Mercy said, ''I'd forgotten about him.''

''Who exactly is Clappman?'' Fitzgerald asked.

''A lawyer, reportedly. Actually he's a trout bum. I think Verlyn pays him with free flies.''

''I'm inclined to like him,'' Fitzgerald said, ''a fly-fishing lawyer.''

''Not if you knew him.''

Jan said, ''I told Verlyn, afterward, that Clappman couldn't handle something like this. We'd have to get a lawyer from Detroit. But Verlyn said all lawyers from Detroit were crooks and I said they couldn't all be and he said they could if you knew Detroit. He can be so stubborn at times.''

''So you said,'' Mercy said. ''How'd it turn out with Stroud?''

''He left, but said he'd be back. Verlyn said he and Clappman would be waiting.''

Fitzgerald said, ''That's when I came in. I ran into Calvin on the river and we decided to have a talk with Verlyn. We thought it might be better, the two of us bringing up what happened to Link. We didn't have a chance. Jan was crying and Verlyn was boiling over Stroud. When I brought Jan over here for a drink he was on the phone trying to track down Clappman.''

"What happened to Calvin?"

"I don't know," Fitzgerald said. "He had something to do." Then he asked Jan if he could freshen her drink again.

"I shouldn't," Jan said, but held out her glass.

"Why the hell not?" Mercy said, and held out hers, too.

LATER, after Fitzgerald had taken Jan home and they made some dinner and then gone straight to bed, Mercy told him how worried she was. He was curled behind her, an arm thrown over her shoulder, breathing into her neck the earthy smell of good whiskey.

"The talk in town, all I heard all day, was that Verlyn had killed Link. And if Stroud couldn't prove it, then Brand would take care of Verlyn himself."

"I know," Fitzgerald said.

"No you don't. That would be even worse. If anything could be."

"Don't worry," Fitzgerald whispered.

"I *am* worried," she said sharply, and turned over, facing him. "Stroud's got to be feeling the pressure. He's got to do something. What choice does he have other than Verlyn? You said you'd help but all you've done is fuss over Jan. Damn it, Fitzgerald, I'm not worried about her.''

She let herself relax then, let her body flow back into his, let him hold her. ''It's such a mess. I don't want Verlyn convicted of murder—and for God's sake I don't want him killed by Brand.''

''I know.''

''Maybe we should talk to Brand.''

''Tell him what? Verlyn's not going to listen to anyone and neither is Brand. The only thing we can do is help Stroud find out who killed Link.''

''Assuming it's not Verlyn.''

''Assuming that.''

''But how?''

Fitzgerald drew her closer, running a hand slowly down her spine, and said, ''I was thinking about the weather. The way it's starting to change.''

''What?''

''In *Walden,* Thoreau's got a section about how spring comes, when it does, all of a sudden. It's just there. You want to hear a line?''

''Not particularly.''

'' 'The change from storm and winter to serene and mild weather, from dark and sluggish hours to bright and elastic ones, is a memorable crisis which all things proclaim. It is seemingly instantaneous at last.' ''

''Now you're memorizing him?''

''Not really. He writes in sentences while most people write in paragraphs. The sentences are so good they stick in my head.''

"And they mean something?"

"That this thing will clear up. That, all of a sudden, we'll understand."

"You believe that?"

"I'm trying to." Then Fitzgerald said, "Trust me a little. I'm doing what I can."

"Oh, I know. But what can anyone do?"

"That," Fitzgerald sighed, "is a good question."

TEN

KIT SAID, "Fitzgerald sucks."

Calvin wasn't entirely sure what that meant in the mysterious slang world of young people. He had heard the expression in New Zealand, so it had international application. He decided to go along with it, cautiously.

"He's got some limitations, that's so."

"Some? What's he ever done?"

"Won the lottery."

"That's shit."

Calvin couldn't argue, and he liked the way Kit put it. But winning one gave Fitzgerald a kind of aura. It set him apart from the fools who paid out hard-earned money and got zero in return. He decided to take another tack.

"He's okay with a rod."

Kit seemed surprised.

"I watched him today. He's rusty from the winter, but he knows what he's doing."

"Mercy thinks he's hot stuff."

"That's another thing," Calvin said. "Your mother's got good taste."

The fire in the stone circle in front of Kit's tent was blazing and the two of them sat as close to it as they could. Calvin felt his face flushed with heat while the cold clung to his back. But it wasn't a bad night as far as temperature went. It was probably one of the better nights the kid had spent in the woods.

In the light of the fire Calvin could see the tent was Verlyn's old Eureka. Kit had gotten bales of hay and placed them around the base for insulation and stacked a couple cords of firewood. It wouldn't be bad in the tent, sleeping, if you went right from the fire to a good sleeping bag and had a wool stocking cap to keep your head warm and maybe a propane heater for the morning when you got back in the bag after going outside to pee.

Calvin had waited until full dark to drive down to the campground at Danish Landing because Fitzgerald said the boy told Mercy, when she first raised a fuss about it, that he only went there to sleep. The rest of the time he was at the Kabin Kamp, taking meals there and working for his father as a handyman and agitating to work in the fly shop during the summer. But Verlyn told Kit he had guides working around the shop when they weren't out on float trips. Besides, Kit had to pay his dues first. That meant he could mow grass during the summer and cut firewood for winter and help the maids clean bathrooms in the lodge.

The boy might listen to you, Fitzgerald had said. *Just talk to him.*

Calvin couldn't believe a kid of Kit's age could have killed Link Pickett. On the other hand, you read all the time about kids, a lot younger than Kit, wiping people out, and for no reason at all. Kit at least had a reason. Or, as Calvin and Fitzgerald had talked about it, you could see why he might have wanted to kill Link.

Verlyn was ragging on Kit all the time, and it was pretty clear the kid couldn't stand his old man and wanted to impress him at the same time. Calvin and Fitzgerald had agreed that all boys probably felt that way about their fathers. And since Verlyn was always bad-mouthing Link, saying he was going to kill him because of the aluminum hatch, Kit might have decided to do it for him. He could imagine it as a way of growing up quick in the old man's eyes.

Talk around it, Fitzgerald had said. *See how the boy reacts.*

Looking at Kit now across the fire Calvin was surprised at how big he had gotten over the winter. He had on heavy clothes but you could see he was taller and had filled out and his face had a more mature look. He was growing a mustache that was still skimpy but had the makings of the real thing. Kit was probably tall enough to look Verlyn in the eye now, man to man. Calvin didn't know if that was a good development or not.

"Fitzgerald thought you ought to go over, you know, see your mother. It was tough what happened."

"So why didn't he come himself?"

"You know," Calvin said, "he wanted to stay with her."

"Mercy can take it."

Calvin said, "You certain about that?" But he didn't want to get into Link's death too quickly. He wanted to talk with Kit first, ease around into it, maybe surprise him into saying something he didn't plan to say.

He got up from the fire and went back to the pickup for a six-pack of Stroh's for Kit and a couple bottles of O'Doul's for himself. He figured Kit would be drinking beer by now since he was Verlyn's son and Verlyn had started sneaking beer around the Kabin Kamp when he was about twelve and hadn't straightened himself out yet. Kit took the beer without saying anything and popped open a can with what looked to Calvin like a practiced hand.

"You could have stayed the winter in my place," he said. "People come in on snowmobiles. I could use somebody keeping an eye out."

"Goddamn snowmobiles," Kit said.

"I didn't have any trouble—nobody broke in, no bears, no red squirrels inside. But you never know."

"You just got back, huh?"

"Half moved in. I got stuff all over the place."

"It must be nice down there, warm and all."

"The fishing's the thing," Calvin said. "New Zealand's got some good rivers. Better shape than here by and large. They pay more attention."

"The Borchard's shit," Kit said.

"Getting to be," Calvin said. "But you can't blame the river. It's the people. They're slobs."

"Anyway, I wanted to stay out here. Verlyn said you and he used to camp all year."

"Down on the South Branch."

"They won't let you camp there anymore."

"It was before the state got the property," Calvin said. "It was owned by some logging company and they'd forgotten it after the trees were gone. You could do anything you wanted down there. Your dad and I had some good times."

"Lucky bastards."

"Except we didn't know it. We were just living. That's how it is. You think back and then, you know, you realize you were having a good time."

Looking at Kit across the fire, seeing his eyes narrowed from the smoke, Calvin realized he was sounding like a wise old philosopher. It was probably how Verlyn came across to his son, and how Fitzgerald did. He had to sound different. Like a friend, but older. An uncle to the kid, which in a way he was. He had known Kit since he was born.

See if he saw anything, Fitzgerald had said. *Maybe heard something. He might have, camping that close to the landing. And another thing. Bring up Link's cutting sweepers. See what Kit says about that.*

BEFORE DRIVING DOWN to Danish Landing, back at his cabin after leaving Fitzgerald at Verlyn's, Calvin had brought up the sweepers with Link's widow.

When Laurel phoned he was arranging his tying

table, getting the materials in the right place so he could reach without looking, his attention while working usually on a Tigers game on the portable black-and-white TV he kept beside the table. He could tie during a game on TV without missing a beat but he couldn't do it with a game on radio. Radio got into his head more than TV, disturbing things. Verlyn, when Calvin mentioned the problem to him, said he was getting to be an old woman. He himself could tie in the dark, doing it all by touch, while Jan gave him a hot-oil massage. Calvin told him he would have to try that, and to send Jan over.

"You by yourself?" he asked Laurel.

"What else?"

"That's good. We don't want any trouble."

"Link's dead, Calvin. I'm his widow."

"Barely," he said. "Let it simmer a while."

He assumed Laurel was calling to set up another meeting at the Keg O'Nails, and probably one that included a session at the motel out back. He wasn't opposed to that, but he was going to suggest that for propriety's sake they drive to Traverse City. He didn't need Willard Stroud thinking what Laurel had thought, that he was the one who took care of Link, and because of her. It might not be easy convincing Stroud the thought had never seriously entered his mind. But Laurel only wanted to talk.

"I'm so mad, Calvin."

"About what?"

"I mean, why doesn't Stroud arrest him? Verlyn

could disappear. He could go to Canada or Mexico—just slip across the border. Murderers do that all the time."

"Look," Calvin said. "Verlyn won't disappear."

"How can you be sure?"

"Because he's got a business and the season's coming. That's how he makes a living. And Stroud hasn't arrested him because he doesn't having anything to arrest him for."

"Link's murder, that's what for."

"Stroud just can't go around arresting people. He's got to have evidence."

"What Verlyn said all the time. That's evidence. You heard him, Calvin. You'll have to testify at the trial. You'll be sworn on the Bible to tell God's own truth."

"They don't do that. There's separation of church and state."

"Whatever," Laurel said.

Listening to her, stroking his beard with his free hand, Calvin heard the same vehemence in her voice he heard at the Keg O'Nails. It didn't sound right. Laurel was usually pretty loose about everything. Maybe it was the prospect of a trial and Laurel imagining herself in the courtroom, a grieving widow wanting justice. She would think of it like the soap operas she watched and wouldn't want to miss playing the part. He couldn't believe she was so worked up over a husband she was two-timing anyway. She was a widow now, free to roam, and with a good business to run on top of it.

"Anyway, it wouldn't just be me. The whole town would have to testify. But that isn't evidence, what someone said. People say things all the time."

"You're on Verlyn's side," Laurel said, the bitterness in her voice unmistakable.

"I don't believe he did it, that's why."

"You work for him, *that's* why. You don't like the canoes any more than he does."

"True," Calvin said. "You ought to turn them in for scrap. But I don't work for Verlyn. I'm a guide who happens to operate out of his fly shop. It's a service he offers people who stay at the lodge. He doesn't get anything out of it."

"Then why do they pay him?" Laurel said stubbornly.

"You know why. It's easier to put my fee on their bill at the lodge. Easier for me. Then I don't have to hassle with people wanting a refund when they have a piss-poor fishing day. Verlyn saves me a lot of grief, billing that way."

"I don't care," Laurel said, "he's still guilty."

"Wait and see," Calvin said.

"That's what I'm telling you. I'm sick of waiting."

"You can't be. It's only two days."

"Long enough."

Calvin had the feeling Laurel was about to break the connection, so he said hurriedly, "Hold on.

There's something I want to ask you. When Link was on the river, what was he up to?''

"Cutting sweepers. Everybody knows."

"That's my point. Anybody with a grudge against him knew he was doing that. They knew he was working his way downstream, cleaning up, and they could figure when he'd reach the sweeper at Danish Landing. You see what I'm saying? Lots of people could have strung wire at that spot."

"Verlyn knows the river best," Laurel said, stubborn to the end.

"Hell," Calvin said, "I know it as well."

"We already talked about you. You said you didn't do it."

"I didn't."

"So there."

KIT KNEW THE RIVER, too. He had fished and floated it since he was big enough to get into waders and handle a paddle. The kid could probably be a guide if Verlyn would ease up on him, forgetting the nonsense about paying your dues first. Camping at the landing, Kit couldn't have missed the big downed sweeper, and he could have calculated the time needed for Link and his chain saw to reach it. Calvin didn't need to ask him about that.

There was another thing. Kit knew about stringing wire in the woods. The thought was in his head. He was still living at home, Verlyn and Mercy still married, when Verlyn strung wire to get rid of snowmobiles on his property.

It could add up, if you wanted it to, and Calvin didn't like the look of the bottom line: Kit was one of the people who could have wiped out Link Pickett.

Calvin opened a second bottle of O'Doul's and glanced across the fire at Kit. The kid was on his third beer, slurping them down like Verlyn would and beginning to look a little glassy-eyed. Calvin had read about the role of genes in human behavior and here was more proof.

"So you weren't around when it happened," he said, getting to the point. With enough beer in him the kid might reveal something. "You were working at the Kabin Kamp during the day."

Kit said. "When I got here Stroud's keystone cops were clomping around in the woods, looking for clues or something. The landing was roped off with that yellow plastic they use. It was like a stupid TV show."

"They were in the woods after dark?"

"That night I got here early. There was light still."

"You talk to any of Stroud's people?"

"I took the road into the campground. I didn't go down to the landing. Why would I talk to them?"

"What I'm getting at," Calvin said, trying to sound careful and off-hand at the same time, "is they're going to want to talk to you. Stroud's going to learn about you camping out here. It's just routine. He's got to check with anyone who might have noticed anything.''

"I told you," Kit said. "I wasn't here when Link kicked off.''

"Before that. It took time to get the wire strung right. It took some figuring. Whoever did it had to know the river and the woods.''

"Like Verlyn.''

Calvin nearly choked on the O'Doul's. He covered his mouth, expecting a fit of coughing, and stared at the kid grinning back at him across the flames.

"Or you.''

"That's not funny," Calvin managed to say.

"Don't get uptight. We both know who got Link.''

"The hell we do.''

"Anyway, Verlyn told me what to do if Stroud comes around.''

"What's that?''

"Shut up and wait for Clappman.''

"Good advice," Calvin said, though he wasn't certain it was.

"Clappman sucks.''

"You could be right.''

Kit asked, "Fitzgerald ever give you some numbers?''

"What?" Calvin said, surprised by the turn in the conversation.

"Verlyn asks him for some. Jan, too.''

"Lotteries are a tax on the poor. I don't believe in them."

"Anyway, I'm going to tell Stroud the truth."

"What?" Calvin said again.

"You know, tell him what I saw before Link hit the wire—somebody in the woods across the river, carrying something. I could see from this side from the high banks." When Calvin's mouth fell open Kit grinned again and said, "Naw. It wasn't the old man."

LATER, WARM in bed under a down guilt, Calvin realized what it meant. He started to get up, to phone Fitzgerald, but then he remembered Mercy would be there and she would have to know who was calling and why. Mercy couldn't leave anything alone. He had to hold the information until morning when Fitzgerald would be by himself, running the risk.

Kit could be in danger.

If the kid told anyone else what he had seen, if it got around, it could get back to Link's killer. The killer didn't know anyone was camping at Danish Landing. He wouldn't have expected anyone this time of year. And he didn't know anyone had spotted him from the high banks of the campground.

You could figure what Link's killer would do if he learned all that.

Calvin wondered if the kid was telling the truth. Kit had said he was only in the campground at night and went to the Kabin Kamp for breakfast in the morning. But when Calvin questioned him he said he had a hangover and slept in that particular morning, so he was in the campground later than usual. He wandered over to the high banks to take a look at the river. That was when he saw the figure in waders in the trees on the other side.

Wide awake now, Calvin got up and tied a few Hendricksons, only half paying attention to what he was doing. After that he read for a while, a book about the native people of New Zealand. When he got back in bed he was able to doze off, but he didn't get a wink of real sleep. The thought kept banging around in his head.

Kit could be in danger.

ELEVEN

PROMPTLY AT NINE forty-five every weekday morning Bonnie Pym left the Six-Grain Bakery in charge of the high school girl who worked part-time on a study-release program and drove a pastry box of assorted sweet rolls to the city-county building. She liked getting a few puffs of a cigarette in the car and talking with the workers in the offices while she distributed the rolls for their coffee breaks. Most of them were girls she had gone to school with who were married and had families and needed two incomes just to get by. The others were old crones who had been in government jobs forever and would die in them.

The office she liked best was the sheriff's. Willard Stroud usually shot the breeze with her for a few minutes, all the while looking her over, usually commenting on her earrings. The earrings had become a thing between them. She wore big, colorful, dangling ones and Stroud made jokes about them putting a lot of weight on her brain but noticing all the same. Bonnie found herself choosing earrings in the morning that were bound to get a rise out of him.

"Like this pair, sugar?" she would say when he

noticed, both of them aware the question covered more than her earrings.

This morning the sheriff's wife, Elsie, was the only one in the office. She was a dried-up mouse of a woman who wore sweat shirts and had blue hair. Bonnie wondered what a man like Stroud, still in the prime of life, had ever seen in a woman as plain and ordinary as that, but she smiled pleasantly and said, "Bank robbery going on, sugar?"

"About as big," Elsie said. She took several rolls from Bonnie's box and arranged them on a glass plate. Afterward she licked icing and jelly from her fingers. "They're all out to Verlyn's."

"Talking to him?"

"Searching. Got themselves a warrant."

Bonnie knew better than to ask what the sheriff and his deputies were searching for at Kelso's Kabin Kamp. You could shoot the breeze around the offices in the city-county building as long as you knew where to draw the line. But the temptation was strong. The search, when the news got out, would be a topic of conversation the rest of the day at the Six-Grain Bakery and Bonnie liked having an item or two of her own to drop into it.

"Wow," she said, and tried to look impressed, "you folks work quick. I suppose you can, easy case like this."

Elsie frowned. "It's not so easy as all that."

"No?"

"Unless they find something out there."

AFTER MERCY LEFT for work Fitzgerald stood with a mug of coffee at the glass-walled front of the A-frame, watching a steady rain soak the pines. The rain was on the verge of sleet, bending the pines down, flattening the whole world. Spring in the north woods was a day of sun and mild temperature followed by weeks of cold rain. Your spirits rose, then plummeted. Thoreau hadn't experienced the touch of depression that could hit you right after breakfast while you watched rain turn to sleet. He hadn't, in any case, mentioned it.

For his own part, Fitzgerald realized, it was going to take an extra effort to get through a north woods spring with his optimism intact. As a starter he went back into the kitchen, opened the whiskey bottle, poured a healthy slug into his coffee.

In the living room he got the light arranged right and settled down at his tying table, thinking to build up a supply of Hendrickson nymphs. The Hendrickson would be the first good hatch of the season if the weather cooperated. He tried to concentrate on that, the season, reminding himself why he was in an A-frame on the Borchard in April in the first place. It had seemed worth doing, spending a whole year on the river and fishing through all the seasons, and still did.

But in the back of his mind on this dripping morning there were questions.

To silence them he asked himself what else he wanted to do with his life. One answer was write his novel, which, winter grudgingly giving way to spring, still held at the planning stage. Another was get a grip on Thoreau, and he had only marginally made more headway with that. He could, of course, sign off on everything, the novel and Thoreau and the seasons, and head back to Detroit and pick up his work.

But he had tried that, and look where it had gotten him. If the lottery hadn't rescued him he would be a smiling boozer with a wife who was tired of him and a career he was tired of himself.

Nothing can rightly compel a simple and brave man to a vulgar sadness. While I enjoy the friendship of the seasons I trust that nothing can make life a burden to me. That was Thoreau for you, always looking on the sunny side. He himself, alas, was neither simple or brave, and he wasn't as immune to vulgar sadness as Thoreau. But he was at least fronting in the right direction. He was still convinced of it.

Detroit was still the wrong direction.

One of the things he did when he moved to the Borchard was quit reading the papers, meaning the *Free Press* and the big-time papers, New York and Chicago. He scanned the *Call,* but that was to keep up locally so he would have something to talk about at the hotel and the Six-Grain Bakery. The surprising thing was he didn't miss the papers at all. For a while he paid attention to National Public Radio news in the morning and again in late afternoon, picking it up on the station in Interlochen, but eventually he drifted away from that, too. Now he just kept music on, not really hearing it so much, just having it in the background.

He felt cut off from the larger world, floating free, and it didn't matter what was happening beyond him.

Thoreau had felt the same way, and to make the point he took some pot shots at the whole idea of news. He said it was essentially gossip—that *they who edit and read it are old women over their tea.* Thoreau had gotten a lot of things wrong, and this was one of them. But Fitzgerald knew what he meant, what he was trying to convey. When he was at the *Free Press* he printed out on his computer Thoreau's line and pinned it to the newsroom bulletin board. He considered it conducive to keeping newspaper work in proper perspective.

He spent a good deal of the time alone in the A-frame on the Borchard, yet he was rarely lonely. His existence had shrunk to a small compass. There was the river, out there beyond the pines, oil-black on a day like this, flowing with impatient indifference on the long journey to Lake Huron. There was the town just upstream, sodden and dispirited in the rain and without beauty, but beckoning him as the day waned.

And there was Mercy Virdon.

He put a size-10 hook in the vise and wound the shank with fine lead wire, giving it weight. Then he cut dyed duck flank feathers as long as the shank and tied them on, leaving a little outward flare. He was concentrating, and pretty successfully. His fingers were loosening up, his eyes getting accustomed to the close work. He was aware of music from the radio and over that sound the sound of rain drumming on the roof, coming down harder than before. But it wasn't intrusive. He wasn't paying attention.

Mercy would have finished two or three Hendrickson nymphs by now, perfect ones. Her fingers were long and thin and they flew around the vise. She was like Verlyn and Calvin. She could keep up a steady stream of conversation and never miss a beat with the fly she was tying. Maybe every good tier on the river was like that. Maybe Nils and Wilma were.

He wasn't. Wasn't yet.

When Mercy said she would think about marrying him it was all he wanted. Probably she guessed that—guessed he didn't want to lose her, that tying good nymphs wasn't the only thing he wasn't up to yet, that he had to go through a year on the Borchard first and finish with Thoreau and make a start with his novel. Maybe even that wouldn't amount to an entirely fresh start in his life. Mercy probably had her own reasons for waiting, reasons he didn't know about and would have to learn. There were always things to learn about a woman.

But some things were certain.

He wanted her with him and he didn't want her hurt and helping her was the same as helping himself.

"Tough on the stomach this time of day."

"Hold the advice," Fitzgerald said, "and start from the beginning." He handed Calvin a mug of coffee, then refilled his own and added a splash of whiskey.

"I didn't want to call last night, Mercy being here. Then, driving over now, I saw the squad cars at Verlyn's and stopped. I would've been here sooner otherwise."

"And?"

"All hell's breaking loose."

"I've got the general picture," Fitzgerald said. "Willard Stroud's at the Kabin Kamp with his deputies. That means he didn't come to talk this time."

"Right."

Fitzgerald sipped his coffee, frowned, and said, "So why's he there, Calvin?"

"Searching the place. Stroud told me himself. Then he told me to clear my ass the hell out."

"Searching for what?"

"He didn't say."

"And Verlyn?"

"You can imagine. He'd called Clappman to get out there."

"Jan's there, too?"

"Stroud's got them both in the fly shop, staying put while the deputies search the lodge and the house. It's no picnic. Stroud didn't have to tell me to get out."

"How about Kit?"

"I almost forgot to tell you. The kid isn't there.

He's probably still in the campground, sleeping it off."

"Wait a minute," Fitzgerald said. "Start over again. Why couldn't you call last night because of Mercy?"

"You got some of that organic orange juice," Calvin asked, "to go with the coffee?"

FITZGERALD LISTENED, saying nothing, while Calvin told him the story. "Kit saw someone in the woods across the river from the campground before Link was killed. He had a good view from the high banks, good enough to see the person was wearing waders and carrying something, though not what it was."

"Jesus," Fitzgerald said. "You should have called anyway. Waiting was a gamble."

"I didn't sleep a wink," Calvin said.

"We've got to get over there, get Kit out."

"The kid was certain," Calvin said. "It wasn't Verlyn he saw."

"He'd say that anyway. But that's not the point. He was in the campground when the wire went up. He saw something. That's the point."

"True," Calvin said.

"We've got to get him out of there, then out of town."

"New Zealand?"

Fitzgerald said, "Get serious, Calvin. It's got to be a place Kit's willing to go."

"He'd go, all right. He knows about the fishing."

"I've got an idea." Fitzgerald sipped his coffee, frowned, and asked Calvin if he would like to be in Detroit on opening day.

"I never miss opening day," Calvin said.

"Not fishing, baseball. The home opener for the Tigers is the first of the week, Monday, and I can arrange for tickets through the sports desk of the *Free Press.* You and Kit can drive down right away. Just take enough time to pack your bags. Spin a story about some business coming up at the Orvis Shop in Southfield—that's why you're leaving right away. They've got a hot idea about setting up fishing trips to New Zealand next winter. Something like that. I'll foot the bill and the two of you can stay in Detroit until I let you know it's safe to return."

"When's that?" Calvin asked.

"Just get Kit out of here. I'll arrange for tickets for the whole opening series. Then I'll try to figure out something else."

"I've never seen Tiger Stadium," Calvin said.

"Here's your chance. Before they tear it down for a new one."

"Maybe the kid won't go."

"All fly fishermen like baseball," Fitzgerald said. "Besides, Kit will go anywhere with you."

"He's got good taste."

"So you get him and I'll get on the phone. Don't say anything to Verlyn or Jan. They've got enough on their minds. I'll have Mercy talk to them later.

She can say we wanted to do something special for Kit. Maybe he has a birthday coming up.''

"I don't know,'' Calvin said. "I was just getting settled in the cabin.''

"C'mon,'' Fitzgerald said. "Anything happens to Kit, you'll be unsettled for good.''

IT WAS THE MIDDLE of the afternoon, rain still drumming on the roof and working now on another Hendrickson weighted nymph, when Fitzgerald got a second idea. But this one he had to discuss first with Mercy.

He called her at the DNR office. "Come on home. I'm not at the hotel bar.''

"Working on the novel?''

"Thinking about it,'' he told her.

He was in the kitchen mixing her a drink when she came in the back door. "Can I take off my boots first?'' Mercy asked.

He led her into the living room where he had started a fire and got her in a chair with her stock-inged feet up on the coffee table and the drink in her hand. "If it's about marrying you,'' Mercy said, "I'm still thinking.''

"What?''

"Try your drink first.''

"C'mon, Fitzgerald.''

"Calvin talked with Kit in the campground at Danish Landing and Kit says he saw someone who might have been Link Pickett's killer. He could see across the river from the high banks—there was someone in the woods carrying something. Wire maybe.''

"Oh, Lord," Mercy said.

"There's more. I arranged for tickets for the Tigers' opening series in Detroit and Calvin and Kit are going down there. Calvin called from his cabin while he and Kit were getting ready to leave. Kit's going along with the idea, though he said he'd believe I could get Tiger tickets for free when he actually saw them. Anyway, all he and Kit have to do is show up at the pass window at the stadium and ask for tickets in my name.''

Mercy said, "You couldn't tell me first?''

"There wasn't time. We couldn't take a chance with Kit.''

"But Detroit. That's scary, too.''

"Not like this.''

"No," Mercy said, and gulped her drink. Then she said, "Tell me again.''

He repeated the story, going over everything, and Mercy kept nodding her agreement. When he was done she said, "You were right.''

"Let's hope so.''

"But now what?''

"That's why I called you. I've got another idea. We can't keep Kit in Detroit forever. We've got to do something to smoke out the killer. So what do you think about this? We float a story that Kit saw someone at Danish Landing just before Link's murder and we get it circulated. Then we see if anybody rises to the bait.''

"You're kidding. Use Kit as bait?"

"He'll be out of town, remember? Besides, we can't keep it secret, his camping out there. It's bound to get around if it hasn't already. So we float the story and I go out and spend a couple days at his camp. Probably nothing will happen."

"Something might."

"Then that's what we want. We'll have the killer out in the open."

"You did on the *Free Press,* float stories?"

"Now and then."

"How?"

"I'll drop the story in Bonnie's ear at the bakery. And I'll tell Nils and Wilma. They'll tell Sandy and she'll tell everyone who comes in the hotel. Then we've got to start working the other end."

"What end?"

"Your friend Laurel. You've talked to her?"

"Just to offer condolences about Link."

"You didn't ask her who else she might have told about the sting?"

"Not then. I couldn't."

"Okay. Try her now. Tell her the story about Kit first, then bring up the other."

"I don't know," Mercy said.

"Neither do I. But I can't think of anything else."

"What you're doing for me," Mercy said, "I didn't expect this much."

"You thought I was only a rich boy."

"I mean it, Fitzgerald."

"I know you do."

"I don't want anything to happen to you."

"Neither do I."

"I don't know. It scares me. If we're going to do it maybe we ought to tell Stroud first." Then Mercy straightened in the chair and said, "Lord, you made me forget."

"Forget what?"

"Stroud searched the Kabin Kamp today."

"I know," Fitzgerald said. "I heard from Calvin."

"He tell you what they found?"

"What?"

"The goddamn wire, that's what."

"IT WAS THE TALK of the town," Mercy explained, "almost as soon as it happened. Everyone thought it was about time Stroud brought Verlyn in. What happened was that Stroud learned the wire that killed Link was the same kind Verlyn used to keep snowmobilers off his property. It seems Stroud kept a note of the make and size of the wire in his files. So he went out to the Kabin Kamp with a search warrant, apparently not expecting much because Verlyn surely wouldn't keep more of the wire around. But it was the only thing he had going for him at the moment."

"And it was there?"

"An entire roll—right in plain view in one of the maintenance sheds."

"Good God."

"By this time Clappman had gotten out to Verlyn's and he told Stroud that in itself the wire wasn't evidence of anything. There were other people who likely had the same kind of wire lying around. But Stroud said it was circumstantial evidence—enough to bring Verlyn in for formal questioning."

"So he wasn't actually arrested?"

"That's splitting hairs as far as the town's concerned."

Fitzgerald was quiet for a while. Then he said, "Either way, it works to our advantage."

"It does?"

"Think about it. If something happens in the campground while Stroud has Verlyn in custody it proves he wasn't involved."

"Oh, swell. Something happens to you and he gets off."

"What I mean is—"

Mercy said, "I know what you mean."

"If nothing happens, on the other hand, it won't look so good for Verlyn."

"I know that, too."

"Let's give my plan a try."

"I still think we ought to tell Stroud first."

"That gets too many people involved. My way, only you and I know I'll be the one in the campground." Then Fitzgerald said, "Two days and two nights. That's all we'll give it."

"And if it doesn't work?"

"We go back to the drawing board."

"I don't know. I wish Calvin was here to go with you."

"He's got Kit."

"Lord, don't you know anything new?" Then Mercy said, "You take a gun with you. That's definite."

"I haven't used one in a long time."

"Then remember how to, damn it."

TWELVE

IN THE MORNING, Mercy gave Fitzgerald instructions about one of her shotguns, a double-barrel 16-gauge she used for bird hunting in the fall. Point and pull the trigger was the essence of it. Then they went over the plan for the day.

Her job was to float the story with Laurel Pickett about what Kit saw from the high banks in the campground at Danish Landing. Link's funeral service was later in the morning at Missionary Baptist in Ossning. Mercy would phone Laurel beforehand to again offer her condolences, then somehow or other drop the information about Kit into the conversation.

"Link as a church member," Fitzgerald said, "that's hard to grasp."

"Don't be silly," Mercy told him. "He wasn't. But any church in town would bury a Pickett."

Fitzgerald's job was to talk with Bonnie Pym, then, later, with Nils and Wilma. In the meantime he would pack some supplies in the Cherokee and be ready to spend the night in Kit's tent in the campground.

"Between now and then," Mercy told him, "you'll have time to work on your novel."

"I don't know," Fitzgerald said. "It might be

hard to concentrate. Maybe I'll tie some Hendrick-son nymphs.''

"Oh, come on. Live it up. Do both. And promise me you'll be careful.''

"I will.''

"I'll kill you if you aren't.''

AT THE Six-Grain Bakery Fitzgerald ate a blueberry muffin and drank three cups of coffee while he waited for the morning rush to end and Bonnie Pym was free to talk.

"Wow,'' she said when he finished telling her about Kit. "That's important, huh?''

"Could be.''

"Willard Stroud will go bananas when he hears.''

"Possibly.''

"But why did Mercy let Kit camp out there? It's too cold.''

"He's a big boy.''

"Hey, don't I know. He comes in now and then.''

"Hands off, Bonnie.''

"Don't worry, sugar. I don't go for boys.''

"You prefer old guys like me?''

"Older and wiser.''

"In that case,'' Fitzgerald said, "there's an impediment. I'm just older.''

Before he left the bakery, Fitzgerald wrote some numbers on the back of cash-register receipt and gave the receipt to Bonnie.

"Lucky, too," Bonnie said, and gave him a wink.

BACK AT THE A-frame, Fitzgerald loaded the Cherokee with what he would need, then waited as the rest of the day dragged on. He went from working on his novel to reading Thoreau to tying flies, succeeding at nothing. He thought about trying for rainbows again, working the same stretch of water he tried the day before, but knew he wouldn't be able to concentrate on that, either. At length, he took up a position at the front of the A-frame, drinking more coffee than he wanted and mindlessly watching the flow of the river below.

When the time at last arrived he drove back to town, this time to the hotel, and parked the Cherokee in front. Inside he chatted with Sandy and drank a schooner of beer while he waited for the crowd of customers at the bar to thin out. Finally, between accordion sets, he got Nils and Wilma alone and floated the story about Kit.

"How come he's in a campground?" Nils asked.

"He's trying to show his father how tough he is. You know the way it is with kids."

"He ought to wait for summer."

"That's the point. Anyone can camp out in summer."

"He's a dumb-ass kid."

"Possibly." Then Fitzgerald said, "But there's nothing wrong with his eyes. He had a good view across the river from the high banks."

"And he got a look at somebody in the woods?"

"That's what he says."

"Somebody carrying something?"

"That's right."

"What?"

Fitzgerald shrugged and said, "I guess Kit's keeping that secret. For now."

Then he asked Nils for a slip of paper, wrote on it, and passed the paper to Wilma. "In case you could use some numbers," he said.

ON THE WAY OUT of the hotel Fitzgerald met Jan coming in. She seemed close to tears and in need of a drink, so he followed her back inside the bar and ordered a double whiskey from Sandy.

"I just can't stand waiting back at the Kabin Kamp," Jan explained, "while Stroud has Verlyn in the city-county building for questioning. It makes me nervous."

"That's understandable," Fitzgerald said.

"So I decided to wait here. At least I'm closer to Verlyn." Then she looked at Fitzgerald and asked, "Am I being silly? I mean, I should probably be home in case he's allowed to call."

"I'd say you're being sweet," Fitzgerald said.

Jan blinked her eyes and leaned close. "Do you think so?"

"Sure."

"You're the one who's sweet."

Fitzgerald gazed at her, trying to gauge the extent of the invitation in her eyes.

"And lucky."

"Tell you what," Fitzgerald said. "I'm going to jot down some numbers for you. Who knows? Could be we both are."

HE TOOK HIS TIME driving downriver to Danish Landing. There would still be enough light when he got there—enough to get settled in Kit's tent, ready for the night.

Then what?

It had seemed like a good idea, changing places with Kit, and it still did. But less so. He could be letting himself in for real trouble. One person had been killed, brutally so, and it was a truism that the first murder was the only one that mattered in a psychological sense. After the first one any others were easy—inevitable, actually.

On the other hand, nothing might happen, in which case the only thing he was letting himself in for was two days and nights of boredom.

So what would it be?

Winning the lottery had been a matter of luck. Dumb luck. But luck wasn't involved now. It was in someone else's hands—someone he didn't know but, if the story he floated with Bonnie and with Nils and Wilma made the rounds, someone who knew about Kit.

Knew about what Kit saw from the high banks.

And where he spent his nights.

THIRTEEN

THE TENT WAS the size of Thoreau's cabin at Walden Pond, give or take a foot or so. It was softly lit inside with pale morning light, and surprisingly snug and warm. Fitzgerald had decided to read for a while before he got up and disturbed the day. So far he had everything backward. The plan was to keep alert during the night and doze in the day, and instead he had slept like a rock until the first rays of dawn.

He opened *Walden* to the chapter about the pond in winter and was beginning to develop some concentration when he heard the snapping of underbrush outside.

He slid the book underneath the cot and eased himself out of it. He crossed the tent floor on his knees to the shotgun propped up against the metal foot locker Kit used for clothes. He had left one of the big side windows slightly unzipped, giving a view of the gravel road coming up from Danish Landing into the first loop road of the campground.

The road was empty, but what he had heard was the sound of underbrush, not gravel. He scanned the wall of woods off to the right. The sound seemed to come from that direction. The woods were cold and sodden, the branches of the pines drooping with morning moisture. No one would come through the woods on a day like this unless they were trying to conceal their presence. If they came that way it wouldn't be for a social call.

He waited, searching the woods, hunting for movement among the pines. Minutes passed. What he heard next was different and coming from the left. He turned to look, and when he did he saw a flash of red.

One thought came to him, edging through the sudden constriction in his stomach: Whoever he is, he doesn't know the place. If he did, and wanted to minimize the sound, he wouldn't come up the foot path from the landing. The surface was loose stone. Coming through the woods, despite the wet pines and the snapping underbrush, would be quieter.

And another thing. He wouldn't wear red.

Fitzgerald lowered himself from the tent window and slid his hand back and forth along the stock of the shotgun. Having it, two shells inside, was a comfort, and he silently blessed Mercy. The second sound came again, off to the left, clearly from the stone of the foot path. He moved back to the window opening just as a figure came from the path into full view on the campground road. He wore a black wool watch cap, bright red parka, and waders. When he saw Kit's Toyota he stopped and looked at it.

Fitzgerald unzipped the front opening of the tent and stepped outside, holding the shotgun across his body. The gun wasn't necessary. Not this time. But it wasn't the sort of decision you wanted to be mistaken about.

"Fitzgerald?" the man called out when he saw him. "Rawlings here. We met before."

Fitzgerald released his breath. He wasn't mistaken. Rawlings had come up the foot path and it was a social call.

Fitzgerald put a hand in the air, a sign of recognition, and Rawlings waved back. When Rawlings came up to the tent he glanced back at Kit's Toyota and said, "When I saw that I thought I was in the wrong loop of the campground. Mercy told me you drove a Grand Cherokee."

"That's so," Fitzgerald said.

"On the other hand, who else would be camping out here this time of year?"

"Mercy told you?"

"She said you were writing a novel. I suppose there's a need for solitude."

Rawlings looked down at the shotgun, curious more than alarmed. Fitzgerald could imagine how it looked—grown man writing a novel in a tent in April with a shotgun for company. He opened the tent flap and placed the gun inside against the trunk. There wasn't any point trying to explain.

"What else did she say?"

"Look," Rawlings said, "I don't mean to disturb what you're doing."

"You aren't."

"I mean it, really."

"You aren't, really."

Rawlings smiled, showing movie-star teeth. He was better looking all around than Fitzgerald remembered from Stroud's office, and the red parka had an expensive Thinsulate-plus-Gore-Tex look to it. The waders were James Scott AirDry neoprenes, top of the line. If he let himself dwell on it, Fitzgerald realized, he could develop a dislike for a man who looked as good as this. Mercy had never mentioned it when she spoke about Rawlings.

"The car belongs to Mercy's son," Fitzgerald said. "Mine's parked in the far loop." He didn't explain why—that the Cherokee was meant to be hidden while the Toyota was the vehicle meant to be seen. "He's the one camping." When Rawlings didn't respond Fitzgerald said, "I'm borrowing his place."

Rawlings nodded. Fitzgerald looked hard to see if there was a hint of a grin on his face but couldn't detect one. "It was Mercy's idea that I should let you know," Rawlings said. "She thought you might notice me here—be surprised in some way."

"I was." Then Fitzgerald said, "Let me know what?"

"The sheriff, if you recall, was concerned that I might have trampled evidence on the day Link Pickett was killed. I don't believe I did. But I've been troubled nonetheless. I telephoned Mercy, asking her to accompany me here. But she was planning to attend Pickett's funeral as the DNR representative."

"Later on this morning," Fitzgerald said.

"It wasn't important that she come with me. I want to see if I can find the trees where the wire was attached. I can find my way."

"Stroud had people out here. They went over everything."

"You miss my point," Rawlings said. "I'm not on a hunt. I just want to see the area again. It might help clear up something I can't get out of my mind. The wire on both trees—I loosened it easily. Do you understand? It wasn't fastened the way you would imagine, not given the purpose someone had in mind. It worked, so to speak. I realize that."

"It killed someone."

"But why wasn't it attached with more care? I removed the wire from both trees in seconds. It stuck in my mind. I think I even mentioned it to Mercy when I returned to where she was waiting with the body. On the other hand, it was a rather hectic situation and I may not be remembering with full clarity. I didn't bring it up with the sheriff."

Rawlings stopped. It was a long explanation— one he had given, Fitzgerald knew, because Mercy asked him to. He wouldn't have explained otherwise.

"Coming out here—I thought it worth a try."

"Sure," Fitzgerald said.

"All there is to it."

Rawlings shifted his weight from one booted foot to the other, anxious to leave. Then he smiled ever so slightly and turned away.

Fitzgerald watched him until the red parka was out of sight. Then he crossed the deserted campground toward the edge of the high banks overlooking the river. By watching Rawlings cross the river he could check out the view Kit had when he saw someone in waders in the woods on the other side, someone carrying something that might have been wire.

Someone Kit said wasn't his father.

FOURTEEN

IT TOOK SOME TIME for Rawlings to reach the road that led down to the landing, then the red parka emerged from the shelter of the pines and Rawlings entered the river and began wading downstream, staying in shallow water close to the bank. The view wasn't perfect. Fitzgerald had to shift position to follow Rawlings' progress, moving from tree to tree, keeping the proper angle.

From the high banks he wouldn't have known it was Rawlings. You had to know a person well— know the clothing they wore, the way they moved, their mannerisms—to make a positive identification from that distance and elevation.

Kit knew Verlyn well enough. Would he have known anyone else?

Rawlings stopped, getting his bearings. Downriver was the big cedar sweeper nearly blocking the stream, the one Link Pickett had wanted to clear. Then Rawlings turned and began crossing the river. He moved quickly, taking the full force of the current on his hip, the water level reaching just above his waist in the middle of the river.

Fitzgerald wasn't familiar with the streambed here. He had fished farther below the campground but not up here—not where canoes cluttered the landing in high season and the campground was filled night after night with noisy canoeists. From the way Rawlings was moving the bottom had to be clear and firm.

When he reached the other side of the river Rawlings hesitated, probably getting his bearings again. Then he stepped up on the bank and began examining the trees, touching them, taking three or four steps into the woods. The red parka was partially obscured now, Fitzgerald just seeing flashes of color among the trees. He was bent down, trying to keep the color in view, when it dropped out of sight altogether.

He knew at once something was wrong.

Rawlings hadn't moved deeper into the woods. He was facing a mottled river birch, examining it. It must have been the tree where the wire had been attached. Then he was down.

Fitzgerald's first thought was that Rawlings had slipped. It was wet and slick in the woods and he lost his balance. It happened all the time. How many times had it happened to him? So he waited for Rawlings to get up, the red parka to reappear among the trees.

But nothing happened. There was no movement across the river. Nothing.

It was quicker to go straight down the high banks, despite the tangle of pine and bare alders, than take the path to the landing. Fitzgerald fell and slid and forced his way through, dropping down until he was at the river's edge. He looked across, locating the mottled river birch, hoping to see the patch of red. Seeing nothing. Rawlings hadn't fallen.

It was something else. And worse.

The river was black and moving faster than it had seemed from the high banks. Fitzgerald stepped in and the water tightened like a vise against his corduroys, the shock of the cold jarring his teeth. He felt a sudden temptation to flatten himself in the water, immerse himself in the cold, know the full extent of it. But that made no sense. He had to keep half dry. And he had to keep moving.

The bottom was firm stone but he took his time, getting the soles of his duck boots planted with each step, balancing himself against the weight of the current. He wouldn't do Rawlings any good if he slipped and was swept downstream. Numbness rose up his legs into his thighs. He lifted his arms, keeping the elbows of his parka out of the water, and kept his eyes on the river birch on the other side, marking the spot.

There was still no movement, no flash of red. Nothing.

The bottom turned to muck as he neared the other bank and he had to lift his feet straight up, the muck sucking against them. His boots were filled with water, sloshing in there, but he had no feeling now. He stumbled getting out and went up the bank on his knees, crawling, grabbing a tree trunk finally and pulling himself upright.

For a moment he lost the birch and pivoted in a half circle, searching.

When he saw it the patch of red was so distinct in the green and brown of the woods he couldn't believe it had been hidden from sight on the other shore. Rawlings was face down beneath the river birch, his body at an awkward angle, as if he had slumped slowly down the tree, grasping it with his hands as he fell, his head thrown slightly back and the black watch cap pushed to one side.

Fitzgerald thought: He banged his head when he slipped. That's why he didn't get up right away. He's stunned. That's why his body looks so awkward.

He pushed through the tangle of undergrowth and reached down for Rawlings' shoulders, meaning to ease him away from the tree, to get him in the open. When his hand brushed against the hard shaft of the arrow he jumped back as if he had touched a live wire.

When he looked again he could see the arrow deeply embedded in the red parka just above the top of the waders. It had entered high and almost exactly in the center of Rawlings' body. He thought: That's how you should do it. If you want to kill someone from behind, that's where you hit them. It's a perfect shot.

Then he knelt down, felt for a pulse on the side of Rawlings' throat, found nothing.

Again he checked, forcing himself to take his time, making absolutely certain Rawlings was dead.

He knew what had to be done. He should disturb nothing, letting Stroud find whatever was to be found. He should leave Rawlings exactly where he was. He should cross the river again and climb the high banks to the campground and drive the Cherokee to the nearest telephone. That would be at High Pines, a convenience store on the South Downriver Road about five minutes from the turn-off to Danish Landing. Then he should come back to Kit's tent and get some dry clothes and wait for Stroud and an ambulance to arrive.

But he didn't move right away.

He stayed hunched over Rawlings' body, keeping very still now, listening for the first time. It hadn't occurred to him before. Whoever killed Rawlings could still be out there. Fitzgerald hadn't seen or heard the arrow. Could you hear one released? Would you notice the flight? He knew less about bows and arrows than guns.

There was another question: Had the arrow come from this side of the river or the other? If it was released from the other side, then the bowman was all the more an expert marksman. The description fit Verlyn. But Stroud had taken Verlyn in for questioning, so it couldn't be him. Besides, lots of people along the river were into archery. Verlyn probably sold as many hunting bows as flyrods.

The only sound now was wind high in the pines. He was safe where he was, but what would happen if he stood up, got back in the river and walked across, made himself an easy target? He remembered the shotgun back in the tent, useless even if he had it. You had to see something before you could hit it. And he had seen nothing other than Rawlings. Heard nothing.

He waited, crouched besides Rawlings, listening, until he could wait no longer. He said a hurried prayer for Rawlings, after that, one for himself, mumbling the words. He hadn't prayed in a long time. Then he began moving.

He crawled through the undergrowth, hands as numb now as his legs, until he was at the river's edge, then slid into the water and straightened up. He planned to keep moving, but the water shocked him to a halt and he stood there, stock still, a perfect target.

He scanned the dense green growth of the opposite bank, rising steeply to the campground. An entire platoon of bow and arrow marksmen could be hidden in there and you wouldn't notice a thing. From the high banks he hadn't seen anyone else cross the river, anyone stalking Rawlings. So in all likelihood the arrow had come from across the river, from the dense growth.

From the direction he was now facing.

The current grabbed at him, pulling him downstream, and he thought for a moment his legs would give way. He would be knocked back into the water. He thrust his boots against the stone bottom, making footholds, forcing his way across while a part of his mind seemed concentrated on a spot high and exactly in the center of his chest.

It was the only part of him that wasn't numb from cold.

FIFTEEN

THERE WAS A catered luncheon at the Pickett home following Link Pickett's funeral. Mercy felt awkward about attending, but when she called Laurel to offer her condolences Laurel insisted she come to the house after the service.

"You're sort of a member of the family," Laurel had said.

It wasn't true. She and Link had been at odds ever since she'd taken over the DNR office in Ossning. What Laurel seemed to have in mind was the fact that Mercy had seen Link die. That didn't make her a member of the family, but it did confer a special status.

At the moment it meant people—all of them Picketts of one sort or other, together with business people from the town—eyed her cautiously over coffee cups and plates of food. They nodded when she glanced their way, but kept a polite distance. Getting close to her seemed to mean getting uncomfortably close to the gory way in which Link Pickett had met his end. Mercy had wondered if the body would be displayed at the funeral service, and felt relieved when, in the sanctuary of Missionary Baptist, she found the coffin firmly closed. It was the sort of queasy weakness she resisted in herself, but she didn't care to have to look at Link again, no matter how deft the work of the undertaker.

"You're the one," she heard a voice say now, and turned to find herself face-to-face with a man of late middle age whose iron-gray hair bristled in an old-fashioned crew-cut. She hadn't heard him come up behind her.

"Could be," she said, "depending."

"I wanted a look for myself and now I've got one."

"Well, good." Then she said, "I don't believe we've met."

"Don't believe we need to."

Mercy was trying to think of something witty to say in return when the crew-cut abruptly turned away and left her for a group of similarly glowering men holding up a wall across the living room.

"Didn't expect you'd be here," said another voice.

It was a bit of a shock finding Brand Pickett at her side, and essentially an unpleasant one. For a moment she couldn't think of anything to say. Brand was the mirror image of Link—a younger Link, and a Link whose hard, dark face was freshly shaved. She couldn't remember ever seeing Link, or Brand, without a stubble of beard clouding their features. Clean shaven, Brand wasn't half bad looking, a thought that had never occurred to her before.

"I was asked," she managed to say. "By Laurel."

If Brand heard the remark it didn't register on his

polished face. Small dark eyes peered angrily at her. "You weren't never on his side. Not one time. You always stuck up for Verlyn."

"I assume you're referring to Link," Mercy said. "And I wasn't on anyone's side. That's not my job."

"You were married to Verlyn."

"Once upon a time."

"It's all the same." Brand seemed to think the pointless remark clinched the argument, one he was conducting with himself. Mercy glared back at him, the unpleasant feeling Brand had stimulated turned to irritation, but the place and time were hardly right for a full-out quarrel. "Nice talking to you, Brand," she said, and turned away as abruptly as the crew-cut had.

"Don't worry none about him," Laurel Pickett said when she came up to her.

"I wasn't," Mercy said.

"Brand's sort of upset. He can't get used to Link being gone."

"I understand." Then Mercy asked Laurel who the middle-aged man had been.

"One of Link's people."

"From here?"

"Somewhere," Laurel said, and waved a hand vaguely through the air.

She was dressed in a long-jacketed navy-blue suit and a frilly ivory blouse—about as near, Mercy had decided when Laurel removed her fur coat in the overheated church during the funeral, as she was likely to come to the colors of mourning. Laurel was usually turned out in the shades of a peppermint stick, if one already well-licked. The image was unkind, but there it was. She had known Laurel all through school and they were friends in the way you were with acquaintances from that stage of life, intimate in some ways without ever being close. Between them, Mercy suddenly realized, there was nothing in common but a common past.

"Suppose we could talk somewhere," Laurel said, "the two of us?" Up close her makeup was as heavy, and as artfully applied, as a stage performer's. After the burial service Mercy had taken time to re-apply her lipstick, but that was the extent of it. The contrast with Laurel left her feeling nearly naked.

"If you like."

Laurel beamed at her, grasped her hand, and drew her down a long hallway off the living room. Mercy felt several pairs of eyes follow her out of view. When Laurel opened one of the closed doors off the hallway they walked into a master bedroom that was a serenade in blue—pale blue carpeting, pale blue walls, two dark-blue wing chairs facing one another across a large colonial-paned window with a console TV set and VCR nearby, dark blue shades on lamps at either side of the bed. The bed was the room's centerpiece—and an astonishment. It was a canopied affair draped with great folds of gauzy white material and plumped with snowy pillows.

"Lord," Mercy blurted out, "Link slept in *that?*" It was hardly the thing to ask under the circumstances, the man not yet moldering in his grave, but the bed had caught her off guard.

"Link?" Laurel seemed to have to summon up her concentration. "His room's across the hall. He snores—" She caught herself and smiled weakly. "Used to."

"It's lovely," Mercy said, trying to make amends. "The whole room's lovely."

"Do you really like it?"

"The house, too."

"You haven't seen it before, Mercy?"

"Well, you know how it is. We're both busy."

It wasn't true as far as Laurel was concerned. She could be seen in summer tending the petunias around the canoe livery, but as far as Mercy knew that was the extent of her involvement with the business. Link and Brand ran it, with assorted nephews and cousins helping out in high season. Laurel Pickett was one of a handful of women in Ossning who didn't have to bring in a second paycheck to keep a family afloat. But she accepted Mercy's polite falsehood with a distracted nod. Her concentration seemed to have drifted off again.

They sat in the two blue chairs by the window, facing one another, Mercy waiting, since the venture into the bedroom had been Laurel's idea. Laurel was the one who wanted to talk. And so did she, Mercy realized, now that the opportunity had presented itself. When she had mentioned to Laurel on the phone that Kit was camping at Danish Landing, Laurel hadn't seemed particularly interested. She didn't seem to grasp the fact that this might have some bearing on finding Link's murderer. Now Mercy wanted to bring up something else.

"Out there," Laurel said before Mercy could begin, "that's because of you and Verlyn."

"What?"

"The way they treated you. They're pretty bitter and all." Laurel paused, making a half-hearted effort to catch Mercy's eye. "I am, too."

"Please," Mercy sighed, "get it straight. The only connection I have with Verlyn is Kit. I'm not responsible for anything he might have done."

"He did, Mercy."

"That remains to be seen."

They lapsed into silence then, both of them looking away, out the colonial-paned window into a winter-bleak expanse of yard. Mercy felt the same irritation with Laurel she had felt with Brand, prompting her to offer some cutting remark before making an abrupt exit from Laurel, the house, the whole Pickett clan. But at the moment she needed information, and a better time might not present itself. When she finally broke the silence Mercy tried for a neutral tone.

"What I'm wondering, Laurel, is what exactly you told Link after I called that day." She plunged on, going over the phone conversation she had with Laurel when she called to alert Link to the sting operation Rawlings planned at Danish Landing.

"Did you tell him just what I said? That we would be waiting for him there? That Rawlings would arrest him when he started cutting the sweeper?"

Laurel nodded.

"And nothing else?"

"There wasn't nothing else to tell."

"So Link was just going to float past the landing. He wasn't going to cut the sweeper. Is that right?"

"Not that time, anyway."

"Okay, now listen, Laurel: Did Link tell anyone else?"

"I don't know."

"Did you?"

When Laurel looked back at her, uncertain, Mercy said, "Did you mention what I told you to anyone other than Link? Did anyone else know Rawlings and I would be waiting for him at the landing?"

"Why would I?"

"It could have slipped out."

"It didn't."

"You're certain? It's important, Laurel. You see, whoever put the wire up—"

"Verlyn did."

"Whoever did it must have known Rawlings and I would be out there. For some reason he wanted us to see what would happen. No one in my office knew, and no one in Rawlings'. That leaves you and Link."

"I can't say for him."

"I know you can't. But let's say he did mention

it—let it slip somehow. It wouldn't have been to Verlyn."

Laurel frowned, creases in her forehead emerging through her makeup like faint etchings on a clay mask. "Link could have told someone else and, you know, it got around to Verlyn."

"I suppose," Mercy sighed. "The other possibility is that it was a pure accident."

Laurel bristled. "It wasn't an accident, Mercy."

"In the sense that the wire was strung at Danish Landing without someone knowing Rawlings and I would be there. That's a whopper of a coincidence. It offends my sense of how things happen."

"I don't know," Laurel said, and turned her head away, seeming to lose the strings of the conversation.

"Tell you the truth," Mercy said, and sighed once more, "I don't, either."

Silence descended again, and while Laurel gazed out at the forlorn yard Mercy found herself contemplating the astonishing bed. She couldn't imagine a wild-boar type like Link Pickett sleeping in something like that—but she could, now that she let herself dwell on it, Laurel. It was totally removed from everything about life in the north woods of Michigan, which was no doubt the point.

Laurel had created a perfect miniature domain for herself. The whole house was involved, with its plush carpets and glittering appliances and pictures on the walls that some interior decorator in Traverse City had probably picked out, but the bedroom was the core of the domain. It was overwhelmingly Laurel's. Mercy could imagine her luxuriating in the canopied bed while Link snored his head off across the hall.

Yet it wasn't the room itself that held her attention. It was what it implied. Laurel had grown up the same way Mercy had—in a house on the scruffy edge of town with tin snow drips on the roof, a wood-burning furnace that never produced enough heat, paper-thin linoleum floors, and too many siblings. Laurel had made her escape into a dream house with an inner retreat all her own—and without a child in sight. Link Pickett was the price, one she had been willing to pay.

Knowing Link, Mercy could imagine it was plenty high. Laurel wasn't about to give up what she had won—and now, Link gone, she wouldn't have to. What she had now wasn't just the room but the entire house. Link was no longer removed to a room across the hall but all the way to the Ossning cemetery. Laurel was, so to speak, home free.

Did that add up to a motive for murder?

The thought rose abruptly in Mercy's mind—unbidden but, like her response to Laurel's outfit, there it was. Had Laurel been willing to kill to extend her domain to the entire house? She was the one Mercy had told about the sting operation at Danish Landing. Rather than telling Link, had she gone out there, alone, and strung a wire across the river? Like nearly everyone in Ossning, Laurel knew the Borchard—and she certainly had access to waders to get herself back and forth. She would have known that Verlyn had strung wire in the woods to intimidate snowmobilers, so by using that method suspicion would fall all the more on him as Link's number-one enemy.

It was possible.

Was it more than that?

"God, Mercy," Laurel said, suddenly breaking the silence, "I need a beer."

"Now?"

But Laurel was already heading for the door while motioning Mercy to stay where she was in one of the blue wing chairs. Mercy was still imagining her traipsing through the crowd of mourners, dressed to the nines and carrying a beer, when Laurel returned with a can of Stroh's Light in hand. She settled back in the second chair, took a long sip of beer, then withdrew a package of cigarettes from her jacket pocket.

With a cigarette in one hand, beer can in the other, Laurel seemed to relax. Even her clay face seemed to soften. "Brand wants me to sell the business," she said. "He brought it up right after Link died. He didn't wait a single day."

"Well, maybe you should."

"Calvin thinks so."

"Calvin?"

Laurel took another long drink of beer and puffed on her cigarette. "That's what I wanted to talk about, Mercy. We've been going around."

"Calvin's been in New Zealand."

"Since he came back. And before."

"Good Lord. It's a wonder you aren't the one dead. And Calvin."

Mercy blurted it out before she could catch herself. But she meant it. If Link had found out, or if one of his innumerable relatives had, both Laurel and Calvin could be in the ground by now. Link might have been willing to sleep across the hall, but his wife fooling with Verlyn's chief guide would have been another matter.

To make certain she said, "Going around, Laurel?"

"You know. Out to the Keg O'Nails when Link was late at the livery or out somewhere."

"Bar or motel or both?"

When Laurel made a feeble attempt at a coy little-girl smile Mercy knew the answer. "You might at least have gone to Traverse City."

"We did a few times."

"Good Lord."

"What I'm wondering, Mercy, is what you'd think of Calvin as a husband."

"Husband?"

"I'm a widow now."

"Rather recently."

"You know Calvin. You went around together."

"Laurel, that was so long ago I hardly remember. Calvin and I used to go fishing. There wasn't much more to it than that. It was how I met Verlyn, through Calvin. If you want to ask anyone, try Bonnie Pym. She knew Calvin best.''

"Who didn't she know?''

"That's so,'' Mercy agreed.

"What I've been thinking is, you know, how it would be. We could be in Ossning all summer and Calvin could work as a guide if he wanted to—''

"He'd want to, believe me.''

"—then we could go down there to New Zealand all winter. I've never been anywhere warm in the winter. Link wouldn't even go to Florida. He liked it up here, doing nothing.''

Mercy stared at her while Laurel took time out to drink and smoke. Here was a new motive, and a different one. It wasn't a house Laurel had in mind but travel—or rather, a house *and* travel. Mercy knew Calvin well enough to be certain he wasn't involved. Calvin and Verlyn were both ecofreaks— a term of derision Link Pickett had liked to direct their way—but that was as far as the similarity went. Calvin wouldn't hurt anyone unless his back was against the wall and there was no other way. If Laurel had killed Link she hadn't done it with Calvin's help.

"If I might ask," Mercy said, "what does Calvin think of all this?''

"We haven't exactly talked about it much.''

"You might let a little time pass—let people get used to the fact that Link's gone. You and Calvin as a pair, it might seem rather abrupt otherwise.''

"I suppose,'' Laurel said dreamily.

"You'd want to get Brand used to it, for one."

"I don't have to pay attention to Brand."

"That's true, theoretically. But he might not see it that way."

"I still don't care."

"And it might be good for Calvin, letting some time pass. After all, everyone thinks his closest friend killed your husband."

"He did."

They had been through that before, Mercy was going to say, when her attention was deflected by the sound of a siren. She listened carefully. An ambulance. Coming from the direction of the river. Heading toward the community hospital. An emergency.

"You all right?" she heard Laurel ask.

Mercy was already rising, leaving the room, leaving Laurel.

"No," she answered.

SIXTEEN

WILLARD STROUD TOLD Fitzgerald the sweet rolls were fresh. Bonnie Pym had brought them in a little earlier from the Six-Grain Bakery.

"Just coffee," Fitzgerald said.

In a patrol car a deputy had driven him back to the A-frame at Walther Bridge for a hot shower and dry clothing, then brought him to town to the city-county building. In the meantime the Tamarack County coroner, Slocum Byrd, had phoned in a preliminary report from the hospital. Rawlings had died instantly from the arrow that had gone into his back high and virtually dead center. There was nothing Fitzgerald or anyone else could have done to save him.

"Whoever fired it," Slocum Byrd added, "was damn good or damned lucky."

"That narrows it down to half the bow hunters in the county," Stroud answered sourly. "And you don't fire arrows. They're released."

Now, a second body on his hands, and this one a DNR official from Traverse City, he knew the media would descend on him in earnest. Grand Rapids, Lansing, Detroit—they might all send in people. The fact that a newspaperman with the *Free Press* had found the body—a newspaperman, on top of it, who once won the state lottery—would add to the attention. The Chicago media might even show up. He needed a talk with Fitzgerald in his office before the story hit the news.

For starters, he wanted to know why someone renting a fancy A-frame on the river happened to be in a tent in the campground at Danish Landing on a cold morning in April.

And why he had a double-barrel 16-gauge with him.

He waited, letting Fitzgerald sip the coffee, both hands circling the styrofoam cup as if he was trying to squeeze warmth out of it. Some color was back in his face but he was still shaky. When Stroud had first seen him, skin the color of chalk and teeth rattling, he only seemed slightly better off than Rawlings. A swim in the Borchard this time of year could have that effect.

Stroud reached for a cigarette, patted his empty shirt pocket, poured himself a cup of coffee instead and broke off an edge of one of Bonnie Pym's sweet rolls. "Okay?" he asked finally.

Fitzgerald nodded.

"Let me understand something. You drove to High Pines, called in, then waited for us there. You could have gone back to the tent and gotten dry clothes. You had a duffel bag there. How come you didn't?"

"I meant to," Fitzgerald said. "Then I remembered Rawlings. I didn't know what was going on. Whoever killed him might still be around."

"After you?"

"I don't know. Why was he after Rawlings?"

"Okay," Stroud said. "Let's go back over everything. Take your time."

Fitzgerald started in again as he had at High Pines, with Rawlings showing up at the tent and saying he wanted to look at the spot where the wire that killed Link Pickett had been fastened to the trees on either side of the river. Fitzgerald added more detail than before but the story was the same. Stroud let him tell it to the end. Then he said, "What did Rawlings mean about the wire? What was wrong with the way it was fastened?"

Fitzgerald shook his head. "Maybe nothing. He didn't know. Something about it just stuck in his craw."

"Goddamn it," Stroud said, "he shouldn't have messed with the wire at all. That was his first mistake. Going out there again was his second."

"He thought, out at the landing, something might come to him."

"And you don't know if it did."

"How could I? He'd only started to look at a tree, sort of examining it, when he went down."

Stroud broke off another piece of sweet roll, chewed for a while, tried to forget he had ever smoked cigarettes. "Let's consider it another way: Let's say Rawlings was right—the wire wasn't fastened to the trees all that well. It wasn't exactly a professional job. What's that add up to?"

"Someone was in a hurry. They didn't take time to do it right."

"But what they did was effective. They took enough time to kill Link Pickett clean as a whistle."

Fitzgerald nodded.

"On the other hand, Rawlings went out there a second time, took a look at a tree a second time, and got killed for his trouble. You might infer he was on to something."

"Maybe not," Fitzgerald said. Then he asked, "Can I have some more coffee?" When the styrofoam cup was filled he held it with both hands again and stared into the steaming liquid.

"Well?" Stroud said.

"This is just a possibility," Fitzgerald said finally. "It might only confuse things."

"They're already confused."

"Maybe Rawlings wasn't the one meant to get the arrow. Maybe anyone out there could have gotten it."

Stroud looked at him hard, eyes narrowed, until Fitzgerald looked back. "Maybe you?"

"Maybe."

"Could be we're getting somewhere," Stroud said. "Now maybe you're ready to tell me why you were in the campground in the first place."

Fitzgerald nodded. "Understand one thing: It was all my idea. Mercy just went along with it."

"I'm all ears," Stroud said.

Fitzgerald went through the story. "Mercy's son, Kit, spent the winter in the campground at Danish

Landing, so he was there, camping, when the wire that killed Link got strung across the river. He could have seen something, and if the killer learned this, he might be in danger. So I asked Calvin McCann to take Kit down to Detroit; I arranged through the *Free Press* for tickets to some Tigers games.''

''Goddamn it to all hell,'' Stroud said. ''You or Mercy should have told me the boy was in the campground.''

Fitzgerald said, ''Maybe, in the back of our minds, we thought you'd learned—that you would have found Kit's tent when you searched the area after Link's death.''

''Searched?'' Stroud growled. ''What search? Who would think anybody was up in the campground?'' Then he said, ''I should lock you all up. You and Mercy and Calvin. The boy's a witness and you're hiding him.''

''Not hiding. You can send a deputy down to Detroit to talk with him. Or Calvin can bring him back. For the time being, though, Kit has to be kept under wraps.''

''Now you're telling me how to do my job.''

''Then I got an idea,'' Fitzgerald went on. ''With Kit out of harm's way but nobody else knowing he was, I could maybe smoke out Link's killer by floating a story around town about Kit seeing someone from the high banks in the campground. Then I'd go out and stay in the tent myself. I'd give it a couple days and nights, seeing what developed. The shotgun was because Mercy was worried.''

"What were you going to do," Stroud said, "shoot anyone who showed up?"

"It was just a precaution."

"You were going to let the other guy shoot first?"

"What I didn't plan on was Rawlings showing up. He told Mercy he was going out there, so she told him I was using Kit's tent—something about doing some writing there. Needing solitude or something. She didn't want us running into one another by accident."

Stroud said, "Knowing you had an arsenal with you."

"Rawlings came up to the tent and we had a conversation. That's when he told me about the wire—what he couldn't figure about it."

"And after that he crossed the river, looked at a tree, and got an arrow in the back."

"Yes."

"But you might have got it, camping there in the tent, if Rawling hadn't shown up. Is that what you're saying?"

Fitzgerald nodded.

"If I locked you up," Stroud said, "one charge would be damned stupidity. Another would be hiding a witness."

"I just wanted to protect Mercy's son. As long as the killer's on the loose he's in danger. I should have checked the whole thing out with you first."

"I'd have told you to forget it."

Fitzgerald said, "But in a sense it worked."

"How do you figure that? What I see is another body and I'm no closer to the killer than before."

"Sure you are. You know Verlyn didn't kill Rawlings."

"How do I know that?"

Stroud stared back when Fitzgerald looked at him. "You had him in for questioning. Because of the wire. He couldn't have been at Danish Landing at the same time."

"The wire?" Stroud said. "Wire like that's all over the county. It's no evidence. I brought Verlyn in to put heat on him, maybe anger him enough he'd say something he hadn't planned to say. I kept him cooped up in the interview room 'til Clappman wouldn't take it any longer. We took him back home last night."

Fitzgerald waited, still looking at Stroud, before he said, "I didn't know that."

"How about arrows? You know anything about them?"

Fitzgerald shook his head.

"The one Slocum Byrd dug out of Rawlings is a Beman. That's high quality—a model called the Carbon Flash. Not many people up here buy arrows that good, but they could if they had a mind to. You following me?"

"Verlyn stocks them?"

"It's better than that. Verlyn once released some arrows over the heads of a party of canoeists paddling past the lodge. He thought they were making too much noise. As you might expect, they weren't happy about that. They complained and I had to go out and have a talk with Verlyn.''

"The arrows he used were Carbon Flashes?''

"You're beginning to get the picture," Stroud said. "You can see why I've got my eye on him.''

BEFORE FITZGERALD LEFT the office Stroud made sure he hadn't changed his mind. "With a second death now, you're still not writing something on the case for your newspaper?''

"If I do," Fitzgerald answered, "you'll be the first to know.''

"We've got an agreement. Right?''

"Right," Fitzgerald said.

"And you're a material witness in Rawlings' death. That means you say nothing to the media without my consent.''

"Agreed," Fitzgerald said.

"One other thing. You remember those numbers you gave me?''

"You didn't win, I take it.''

"Feel like trying again?" Stroud asked him.

MERCY SAID, "I think I knew what it was the minute I heard the siren. But my first thought was you. Lord, I thought, that stupid idea worked and now he's dead. Rawlings never came into my mind.''

After she picked up Fitzgerald at the city-county building he asked her to take the South Downriver Road to Danish Landing so he could return the Toyota to the Kabin Kamp, where Kit had left it when he and Calvin took off to Detroit in Calvin's truck. Fitzgerald had brought the Toyota to the campground, and he didn't want to leave it when no one was around to keep an eye out. Then Mercy could take him to the High Pines convenience store, where the Cherokee was still parked in front. After that, it was home and some decent coffee. When Mercy asked if he felt good enough to drive, he said he felt fine.

"From Laurel's house I went to my office," Mercy said, "but no one had heard a thing. That's when I phoned Stroud. Lord, Fitzgerald, I felt relieved when he told me. I know that's terrible."

"I'm glad you did."

"After I talked to Stroud I called the DNR office in Traverse City and broke the news. They didn't know Rawlings was even in Ossning. He hadn't told anybody what he was up to." Mercy paused, both hands gripping the wheel of the Suburban, her face taut with the effort of control. Fitzgerald thought she had never looked so good. "Rawlings had a wife and two children."

"That's rough."

"It's godawful hell." Then she asked, "You want to talk about what happened?"

"When we're home."

"You sure you're all right?"

"I'm sure."

"It's strange," she said. "Here I'm worrying about you just the way you were worried about me."

"It's strange," he agreed.

"But it's nice to have someone worry."

"It is."

"If I wasn't driving, Fitzgerald, I'd kiss you right now."

"Pull over a second."

THEY DIDN'T NOTICE IT until they parked the Cherokee and the Suburban side-by-side and were walking together to the back entrance of the A-frame—the glass from the storm door littering the wooden steps of the house. Fitzgerald held Mercy back with his arm as they stared at the open inner door leading to the kitchen, then he motioned with his head and she went back to the Suburban for the service revolver she kept in a locked metal container under the front seat.

Together they went up the steps, then waited in the entry to the kitchen, crouched down, listening. The only sound they could hear was the hum coming from the refrigerator. The kitchen seemed undisturbed. They waited some more, then edged their way through the kitchen and along the hallway that led to the living room.

What they saw there was another story.

The room had been ransacked. Books were dumped on the floor, the fly-tying table overturned and materials scattered, the mounted sailfish torn off the fireplace and broken in two. Fitzgerald's first thought was about how he was going to explain the busted trophy to the Old Kent Bank, his second for the spare bedroom where he had his desk and he and Mercy kept fishing equipment. He motioned to her and they went back down the hallway, Mercy in front, revolver drawn.

The doors to both bedrooms were flung open—and both rooms were in shambles.

In the spare bedroom his laptop computer had been smashed against a wall. Waders and fishing vests were slashed with a knife or razor. Rods had been removed from cases and broken into pieces.

"Lord," Mercy said, breaking the silence, "the novel. It was in there?" She was standing over the laptop, the revolver dangling by her side.

"Only notes," Fitzgerald said. He reached down and picked up a piece of a Sage rod. It didn't seem to matter any longer whether someone was still in the house.

"Wait here," Mercy said, and left the room. When she came back she said, "It's clear. But I don't get it. There's money left on the bureau."

Fitzgerald held out the shattered piece of rod. "It wasn't robbery."

"Should I phone Stroud?"

"You should, but don't. Let's make the coffee first and think this through."

"I'm sorry about the notes."

Fitzgerald shrugged. "The rods hurt more." Then he said, "He doesn't know we like good coffee or we'd have a busted kitchen, too."

"Why do you say 'he'? Stroud always does, too."

"A woman wouldn't make a mess like this."

"Probably not," Mercy agreed.

THEY SAT AT the trestle table in the kitchen and sipped the coffee Fitzgerald made. He had added whiskey to both mugs.

"What are you thinking about?" Mercy asked him.

"Thoreau."

"Now?"

"When he had visitors at the pond, people who came when he wasn't home, they left flowers or evergreen wreaths as calling cards. Some wrote their names in pencil on walnut leaves or wood chips."

"You're trying to tell me something?"

"I'm not sure."

Mercy said, "It might have been kids—you know, just raising hell."

"And it might have been whoever killed Rawlings. He could have come from Danish Landing to here. He could have known you were gone during the day and I'd be tied up with Stroud."

"But why?"

Fitzgerald got up from the table, refilled their mugs, added more whiskey. "Only a guess," he told her.

"Well?"

"To leave a message."

SEVENTEEN

FITZGERALD TOOK HER step by step through what had happened in the campground at Danish Landing, the same story he told Stroud. Then he told her about Verlyn—that Stroud had released him and about the kind of arrow used to kill Rawlings.

"So what?" Mercy said. "The arrow's no better evidence than the wire. Other people use Carbon Flash and other places sell them."

"There's something else," Fitzgerald added. "Something I didn't tell Stroud. I thought it might be too dangerous. Now I'm certain it is."

"For God's sake, what?"

"Before I heard Rawlings come up the path from the landing I heard something else. Someone was moving through the woods, snapping the underbrush. I'm positive the sound didn't come from the same direction as Rawlings."

"Maybe an animal."

"Could be. But let's say it wasn't. Let's say it was someone approaching the campground through the woods at the same time Rawlings was coming up the path from the landing."

"But Rawlings would have seen another car at the landing. And if anyone had driven up into the campground you'd have heard it."

Fitzgerald nodded. "So whoever it was parked somewhere else and walked in. How far is the next landing?"

"Two or three miles by road. But there's another way he could have come—downriver by canoe."

Fitzgerald shook his head. "I don't think so. It would be too easy to be seen. He'd have to pass too many cabins. My guess is he walked through the woods from the next landing."

"That's another whopper of a coincidence—getting there the same moment as Rawlings."

"But it must have happened. Whoever it was arrived at the campground at daylight, just like Rawlings. Rawlings never saw him, but he saw Rawlings. It wouldn't have been difficult. Rawlings came up the path in waders and a red parka, then he called out to me and I came out of the tent. Whoever it was must have been surprised. He'd kept himself hidden in the woods."

"Okay," Mercy said, "let's say all that. But why was he there in the first place?"

"The reason we thought."

"Kit?"

"I think so. He must have been waiting for enough light—"

"And when there was movement inside the tent he would have released an arrow. Or maybe he was waiting until you stepped outside. Good Lord, Fitzgerald. You could be the one dead. Or Kit."

"But he didn't. He didn't do anything."

"Because Rawlings happened to be there."

"That was probably the first reason. The other was what he heard Rawlings say. He changed his plans on the spot. He decided there was someone else he had to kill."

"All Rawlings said was about the wire—the way it was fixed."

"That was enough. The person followed Rawlings when he went back down the path to the landing. He knew I was still in the campground—maybe he saw me on the high banks, watching Rawlings cross the river. So he had to keep to the woods, had to keep silent. Following Rawlings that way, through the woods, then finding a hidden but open spot where he could release the arrow—it means he's someone who knows his way around that part of the river."

"Which includes me," Mercy said, "and a couple dozen others I could name."

"Let's keep on this track," Fitzgerald said. "What Rawlings said about the wire caused his death. That means I was in danger, too. I heard what he said. The killer could have hit me with an arrow when I crossed the river to try to help Rawlings. It would have been easy. So the fact that he didn't suggests he was in a big hurry to get away after hitting Rawlings. Or—"

"Or what?"

"He thought he could take care of me another way."

"How?"

Fitzgerald spread his hands. "Like this. By trashing the house. Intimidation. And that includes you. Rawlings told you, before, what he told me about the way the wire was fastened to the trees.''

''I don't even remember.''

''I don't think it matters. The killer heard what Rawlings said, that he'd mentioned the wire to you. That's what matters.''

THEY DRANK more coffee with more whiskey in it, both of them quiet now, thinking. Finally Mercy said, ''So, if you're right, we're both in danger. Where does that leave Kit?''

Fitzgerald said, ''We have to assume he's in danger as well.''

''You didn't tell Rawlings he was in Detroit with Calvin?''

''No.''

''Then we just have ourselves to worry about.''

''Maybe not even that. The house, the mess it's in, was meant to scare us off. At least that's a theory. The killer doesn't want to kill anyone else. He wants to end it with Link and Rawlings.''

''Assuming Link and Rawlings were killed by the same person.''

''Assuming that.''

Mercy said, ''Let's call Stroud. Tell him everything—about the house, about someone in the campground besides you and Rawlings. We've fooled around long enough.''

Fitzgerald didn't respond right away, his chin propped up with a hand, looking back at her without seeing. Then he asked her, "Have you changed your mind? Do you think Verlyn killed Link, then Rawlings to cover up the first killing?"

Mercy shook her head. "It doesn't make sense. Stroud lets him go and right away he kills Rawlings with the kind of arrow everyone knows he uses? Verlyn couldn't be that dumb—or, for that matter, that calculating."

"Stroud feels otherwise," Fitzgerald said.

"Of course he does. Verlyn's the only suspect and the town wants his hide."

"Then if you still want to save that hide we'd better keep working on our own."

Mercy sighed and said, "So what do we do?"

"Let's think about what Rawlings said about how the wire was fixed to the trees. He didn't think the job had been done carefully enough if the intention was to kill Link. Let's say he was right. What does it tell us?"

"That the killer was in a rush, though not so big a rush the wire came loose or went slack. But what does *that* tell us?"

Fitzgerald said, "I'm asking you."

"Or maybe it tells us he's a she. Women are notoriously jumpy under pressure. Isn't that the going view?"

Fitzgerald looked at her across the table. "You brought that up before—a woman. Anyone particular in mind?"

Mercy shrugged. "Only Laurel, I suppose. There was a luncheon after Link's funeral and Laurel took me into this blue bedroom with a frilly canopied bed. Link probably never set foot in the room. I got the feeling Laurel would do about anything to protect, and maybe enlarge, the place she'd created for herself. Who knows? Maybe having Link off in a bedroom of his own wasn't enough. Maybe she wanted him in his grave.''

Fitzgerald said, "I thought Laurel was a sort of pretty bubblehead."

"Don't kid yourself. I could tell you things. Laurel and Calvin, for one. They've been together out at the Keg O'Nails and in Traverse City."

"Recently, you mean?"

"Before Calvin went to New Zealand and since he's been back. Laurel told me she was even thinking of marriage. When I protested that she might be jumping the gun—let alone what Calvin might think of the idea—she told me she was, after all, a widow. So I suppose that's a motive—Laurel wanting Link out of the way so she'd be free to marry Calvin."

"She could have done it?" Fitzgerald asked. "She's familiar enough with Danish Landing?"

"And nail Rawlings from across the river with an arrow from a compound bow? Damned right she could."

"But she was at Link's funeral when Rawlings was killed."

"I know that," Mercy said. "There might have been enough time beforehand to get to the landing and back. Maybe everybody thought she was secluded in that blue bedroom—and she just slipped out. The funeral was perfect cover. Who would suspect her of being anywhere but there?"

"That means Laurel was acting on what you told her about Kit—that he saw someone at the campground. She didn't go out there intending to kill Rawlings. It was your son she was after. Is that what you believe?"

Mercy said, "I don't know what to believe."

FITZGERALD WAITED, letting Mercy sip her coffee, letting her ponder Laurel Pickett as the killer of her husband, the killer of Rawlings, the one who had meant to kill Kit. She frowned and rubbed her eyes and squirmed in the chair. At length she said, "There's someone else we have to consider."

"Not Calvin," Fitzgerald said. "Not just because he and Laurel were having a fling. If they really were."

"Why would Laurel lie about it? And of course not Calvin."

"Who then?"

"Brand, that bastard. He came at me at the luncheon after the funeral. But it was odd, like it was a set up—first Link's crew-cut relative singles me out for abuse, then Brand. I can understand that Link's people would hardly want me around, given that I was married to Verlyn, the one they think killed Link. But I saw Link die and helped haul his body out of the river and waited with it until Stroud arrived. I didn't expect gratitude because of that, but you might think Link's people would at least be civil toward me, especially during the funeral luncheon.

"But Brand went out of his way to be uncivil, which maybe only proves he's a Pickett through and through. But it might indicate something else—that he was trying to establish an alibi for himself. I'd remember talking with him, and if he was at the luncheon after Link's funeral then he couldn't have been at Danish Landing sending an arrow into Rawlings. On the other hand—"

"What?"

"That alibi doesn't hold water any better than Laurel's. Brand could have been at the landing earlier and slipped back in time for the service. His reasoning could have been the same as Laurel's. No one would suspect him of anything on the day of his brother's funeral. Still and all—"

"What?"

"Why would Brand have killed Link, let alone Rawlings?"

"You tell me."

Mercy said, "The only thing I can think of is what Laurel said—that Brand wanted to buy Link's part of the canoe business. Maybe Brand's greed was stronger that his familial affection."

"Maybe," Fitzgerald said doubtfully.

"You don't believe brothers kill brothers?"

"Not over a canoe business."

"Spoken like a true fisherman. C'mon, Fitzgerald. Brand had a motive."

"So did Verlyn and Calvin and Laurel."

Fitzgerald stood up, stuck his hands into the pockets of his corduroys, began pacing the kitchen.

"I take it you're thinking," Mercy said.

"That we're not going to get anywhere until we figure out about the wire. Why was it strung at the place you and Rawlings were waiting? Why plan to kill Link there, with eyewitnesses? And why does it matter how the wire was fixed to the trees? It's significant—that's the one thing we know for sure. It got Rawlings killed. But why?"

Mercy sighed and said, "I think we're repeating ourselves."

"Got a suggestion?"

"No, but let's go in and look at the mess again. Let's feel sorry for ourselves."

Mercy was in the middle of the living room, looking it over, when she saw the red light blinking on the telephone answering machine. "Fitzgerald," she called out, and pointed at the phone. "I never noticed it. All the confusion—"

Fitzgerald said, "That makes two of us."

"It could be Calvin. Or Kit. Maybe Stroud."

But when Fitzgerald pressed the PLAY button a voice Mercy didn't recognize said, "Walker Berry here. *Free Press*. I'm in Traverse City at the moment, on my way to Ossning—working on the murder of the DNR fellow. I'm wondering if we could get together. I'll be at—"

"You know him?" Mercy asked when the message ended.

"Some."

"You'll see him?"

"I'm on leave," Fitzgerald said. "He can earn his own living."

"Generous of you."

"And I gave Stroud my word I wouldn't get involved."

The machine clicked back on then and they heard a second message—and a voice they both recognized. "We got us a problem," Calvin McCann said. "Call me."

They looked at each other for a moment before Fitzgerald dialed the number Calvin had given, one with a Detroit area code. The phone was answered after one ring.

"I've been sitting here," Calvin said. "What took you so long?"

Fitzgerald launched into an explanation that was meant to include Rawlings' death and the trashing of the A-frame, but Calvin cut him off. "It's the kid."

"What about him?"

"The little shit," Calvin said. "He took off."

EIGHTEEN

MICHIGAN SUCKS. The only good thing about the state was the Borchard, and that was going down the tubes. Verlyn and Calvin said twenty-inch browns and rainbows used to be common in the river, now you were lucky to hook one a season that size.

On the other hand, Verlyn and Calvin were full of it. You couldn't believe a word they said.

Kit wondered why he stayed in such a crummy state. Why didn't he go out to Montana and find a place to live near the Madison, or go down to Colorado near the South Platte? Or to New Zealand? According to Calvin, twenty-inchers were a nuisance in New Zealand. He had no excuses for Montana or Colorado, but he hadn't gone to New Zealand because Calvin hadn't asked him.

Calvin only asked him to go to crummy Detroit.

Which hadn't turned out too bad. Calvin said Cecil Fielder could be in the Hall of Fame someday, and maybe Trammell and Whitaker, and Sparky Anderson might make it as as manager, and Kit could say he saw the team they were with. Calvin had a funny way of looking at things. Those guys *used* to be with the Tigers, replaced now by a bunch of no-names.

But he had felt some excitement anyway. The weather was football weather, forty degrees and no sun, yet the opening game was well played and Kit found himself yelling his head off when one of the no-names hit one in the upper deck to put the Tigers ahead for good.

The motel they were staying in was somewhere out in Southfield, a million miles from the stadium, but it wasn't a bad place. The television had about a hundred channels. Calvin said he wouldn't stay in Detroit because of the crime, and he wouldn't stay anyplace where he couldn't park his pickup at the front door. He also said he had some business at an Orvis shop, something about guide trips in New Zealand next winter. Calvin was at the shop the next morning before the second game that afternoon, Kit still in bed at the motel, when the call came.

Actually, it was the lower half of the state that sucked. Along Interstate 75, where he was at the moment, it was all industry and strip malls and even the plowed farm fields you saw had probably been toxic dumps. You had to get north of Saginaw Bay to find halfway decent country, and it still wouldn't feel entirely right until you reached Higgins Lake and were back again in jack pines.

Now, at a truck stop just outside Flint, the air smelled like a combination of cooked cereal and leaking propane. Coming down through Flint on the way to Detroit, Calvin had told Kit to breathe as shallowly as he could, which was bullshit advice, for the more he tried that the more he took deep breaths, gulping poison into his lungs.

He hadn't wanted to take off on Calvin. He would be totally pissed when he found out, which meant Kit would get a hard time all summer and Calvin wouldn't let him hang around with the guides in the evenings and listen to the talk. He would never learn the guide business otherwise. Sure as hell he wouldn't learn it from Verlyn. All Verlyn did anymore was hole up in the fly shop during the day, tying flies and running the cash register, then go out at night and fish spots on the South Branch that he and Calvin kept secret.

But after the call Kit didn't have any other choice.

Stroud had Verlyn in jail for killing Link Pickett and Kit was the only one who could save him. Even though he was trying hard not to breathe the Flint air he had to grin at the thought. Nothing he could do would needle Verlyn more.

Kit hadn't wanted to get into a hassle with Calvin about going back, which is what would've happened if he'd waited at the motel until Calvin returned from the fly shop. And he didn't want to explain. Explaining would ruin everything. So he left Calvin a note. The idea was to get to Ossning, get his Toyota from where he left it at the Kabin Kamp, tell Stroud his story and sign a statement or whatever Stroud wanted, then whip back to Detroit and meet Calvin for the third game of the opening series.

If he went to another ball game with him Calvin might not be so sore. He wanted to stay on Calvin's good side. Calvin's way of guiding was to let people go fishing with him rather than bow and scrape and get uptight about everything the way some guides did. Calvin didn't give a damn whether people caught fish or whether they had a good time. They got their money's worth watching him fish and have a good time.

That was the kind of guide Kit wanted to be, and he wanted to hang around Calvin long enough to learn the tricks of the trade.

He picked up the sign he had scrawled on the bottom of a Domino's pizza box—NEED RIDE TO OSSNING—and hunted for a new position in the truck stop, one nearer the entrance road to the Interstate. Where he was now a million trucks were parked with their motors running, fouling the air even more. He had good luck getting out of the Detroit area, meaning he got rides without too much waiting and hadn't been picked up by a serial killer, but Flint was turning into a big blank.

He pulled the stocking cap down around his ears and fastened the top button on his parka. He had on the winter clothes he wore for camping at Danish Landing but he could still feel the cold, reaching inside, fingering his skin. Once he got north of Higgins Lake, if he ever did, he wouldn't feel it anymore. It would be a different cold then.

The cold of the part of Michigan that wasn't half bad.

"HOW DO YOU MEAN 'took off'?" Fitzgerald asked on the phone.

Calvin said, "What else is there? I get back to the motel, he isn't here, there's a note. He says Jan called and he's hitching a ride back home for something he has to do. He'll be back for tomorrow's game."

"Something?"

"What he says."

Over his shoulder Fitzgerald told Mercy what Calvin had said and she said, "How could Jan call him? She doesn't know he's there."

"I heard her," Calvin said. "I think I know."

"Well?" Fitzgerald said.

"I told her."

"Jesus, Calvin, you weren't supposed to tell anybody."

"Yeah, but Jan's sort of his mother."

When Fitzgerald told her over his shoulder Mercy snapped, "Damnit, Calvin. Sort of his *stepmother*."

"I had to take Kit over to the lodge to get more clothes. He didn't have enough clean stuff at the tent. Jan, she wanted to know what was going on, so I told her we were going down for opening day. That you'd got tickets."

Mercy said, "Ask how she knew where they were staying."

"I heard her," Calvin said. "I told Jan it would be someplace in Southfield because I had business at the Orvis shop. She must have called around."

"Now listen," Fitzgerald said. "How long has Kit been gone? Figure it out."

"I already did. Three hours max."

"Okay. See if you can find him. Take the same route you took driving down. If he's out hitching you might spot him. If you do, get him back to Southfield and keep him there. Tie him up if you have to. You understand, Calvin? Mercy and I'll hunt for him on this end. We've got to find him."

"What should I do about the tickets?"

"Jesus," Fitzgerald said, "whatever you want."

"Anything new up there?" Calvin asked.

"Brace yourself," Fitzgerald said. "Plenty."

He gave Calvin a quick account of Rawlings' death and the fact that Verlyn had been released beforehand by Stroud. "That means he's now a prime suspect in two killings. And, there's something else: When Mercy and I got back to the A-frame the place was trashed. We took that to mean that we were given a warning, either quit nosing around or expect an arrow in the back."

Calvin asked, "They get the fish on the fireplace?"

"We can't keep talking," Mercy told Fitzgerald. "Tell him to get moving."

"I'm off," Calvin said.

"This is important," Fitzgerald said.

Calvin's voice on the other end of the line was as somber as Fitzgerald had ever heard it. "You tell Mercy to take it easy."

"Sure," Fitzgerald said.

After he hung up he glanced at Mercy, then looked away. There was too much worry in her face.

"How many times do you have to tell them?" Mercy said. "Never hitchhike."

"I know," Fitzgerald said.

"No, you don't. All you have is an ex-wife." Then she said, "The only woman I thought about was Laurel. I forgot about Jan."

"What?"

"It's possible."

"Come on. Jan's not the type."

"What type? You don't think she could handle a hunting bow? Or that she's all sweet and meek and thinks only about fixing her hair? Think again."

"But why?"

"I don't know why. Maybe she's sick to death of Verlyn. Maybe she wants to own the Kabin Kamp. Believe me, underneath the safari suit Jan's as tough as nails."

Fitzgerald said, "Think about it. What you're suggesting is that Jan knew Link was going to be on the river and went out to Danish Landing and strung the wire, knowing Verlyn would be the main suspect. Then she heard about Kit staying at the campground, so she went out there to kill him, too, and ended up killing Rawlings. Is that what you mean?"

"Maybe I do."

"Well, there's a problem. Jan already knew Kit

was at the campground. She didn't have to learn about it. And if she knew he was there, why risk stringing the wire where he might notice? Why not elsewhere?''

''Because that's where the sweeper was. Besides, maybe she only knew Kit was camping out. Maybe she didn't know where. You know Kit. He won't tell you anything if he doesn't have to.''

Fitzgerald started to respond, then stopped and looked hard at Mercy.

''Well?'' she asked him.

''I just remembered something. When I went to the hotel to float the story about Kit seeing something at the campground, Jan was there. Stroud had Verlyn in for questioning and she said she couldn't wait at home. She wanted to be close to him. After I left she could have heard about Kit from Sandy.''

Mercy said, ''You see? Call Calvin back.''

''What for?''

''I want to ask him if he's been seeing Laurel.''

''You said she wouldn't lie about it.''

''To make sure she wouldn't.''

But when Fitzgerald placed the call there was no answer.

''Damn it,'' Mercy said. Then she said, ''But he's looking for Kit.''

CALVIN DIDN'T THINK it was legal to hitch on the Interstate, and it was too cold to hang around entrance roads. So he reasoned Kit would try to bum a ride at a truck stop. He had seen kids at those places with signs saying where they wanted to go.

But what truck stop?

Calvin went through them one by one after he got north of Pontiac, cruising the parking areas first and then going inside to look through the restaurants. He ordered a take-out de-caf coffee at the counter, feeling he ought to buy something to keep from arousing suspicion, and checked out the waitresses, but he didn't allow himself to waste time. Kit had been his responsibility. He was supposed to keep the kid down in Detroit and out of trouble and he hadn't gotten the job done.

Calvin could feel something resembling guilt weighing down on his shoulders. That could happen when you got too involved in other people's lives. He made a mental note that, once this was over, he would put some distance between himself and the kid.

The same went for Laurel Pickett.

On the way to the next truck stop he thought back over the night at the Keg O'Nails when Laurel told him about Link. She wanted to know if he had killed her husband. But it was only talk. She had already made up her mind that Verlyn did the job. So why had she brought it up at all? Just because she thought it would be nice if he *had* killed Link? That didn't make sense.

But another thing suddenly did: Laurel had done the job herself and had been trying to shift attention elsewhere—to him, to Verlyn, to anyone available.

The thought hit Calvin hard, tightening his stomach for an instant, and he had to grip the steering wheel with both hands. It wasn't the possibility that Laurel was a murderer that was so wild. He could imagine her stringing wire at Danish Landing in order to wipe out Link—and, after that, he could imagine her putting an arrow in the DNR man, the one who was Mercy's boss, to cover up the other killing. What was so wild was her reason for the killing—the first one.

So she would be a widow and free to marry him.

At the next truck stop Calvin ordered a take-out tuna on pita bread to go along with the de-caf coffee. Time was draining away from his search for Kit but he needed food to steady his stomach.

DARKNESS HAD FALLEN by the time Kit reached Ossning. A trucker who hauled logs for Weyerhaeuser back and forth to Bay City took him along South Downriver Road to Walther Bridge and Kit walked the rest of the way to the Kabin Kamp.

Weyerhaeuser really sucked, clearcutting all the timber it could get its hands on, and Kit hoped nobody he knew saw him get out of the truck. Verlyn would have had a heart attack. Calvin, too. But the trucker had been okay. He was willing to drop Kit in the center of town or Walther Bridge, either way, and Kit had decided he'd get his wheels first before he saw Stroud and then headed from town straight back to Detroit.

The lodge and the fly shop were dark beyond the

halogen lights that illuminated the parking area, but through the trees Kit could see lamps lit in the house. He headed for the garage building where vehicles were parked, then turned and went toward the house. There was something funny about the lights. Unless Jan had left them on as a precaution, why were they on at all?

An open porch extended across the front of the house and he took the steps to it quietly. He went along the porch to the living room windows, going on his knees the last few feet, and looked inside. There was Verlyn, sitting at his tying bench, the television going, tying flies and watching some dumb movie at the same time.

What the hell?

Verlyn was in jail. Jan had told Kit that on the phone. She said Stroud had taken him in for the murder of Link Pickett. Clappman was working to get him out but it would take time, and in the meantime Jan said she didn't know what to do. The only thing she could think of was to call Kit. She hated to spoil his vacation in Detroit, but she knew he would want to know. Maybe he would want to return home to be close to his father.

He wasn't on vacation, Kit told her. He was seeing some ball games with Calvin. And what difference did it make whether he was close to Verlyn if Stroud had Verlyn in the tank? But Jan was half-crying and half-gushy and you couldn't hold a conversation with her.

Not that he had wanted to. The act hadn't fooled

him for a minute. All along he could hear another voice, the real one, beneath what she was saying.

So he figured Jan would be gone. She wouldn't hang around the house, and he had a pretty good idea where she would be. But why was Verlyn out of jail? Had Clappman sprung him on bond or whatever it was lawyers did? Kit took another look at Verlyn through the window; he didn't seem like someone who had just had a murder rap hung on him; he looked happy as a clam.

Kit had to hand it to him. If Verlyn had wiped out Link, which he probably did, he was damn cool about it. And the bastard could tie flies. Sometimes, watching Verlyn tie or watching Calvin, Kit had the feeling life was hopeless and he ought to go back to Central Michigan and study accounting or some other dumb meaningless thing.

He turned away from the window and went back along the porch on his knees until he got near the steps. What was he going to do now? If Verlyn was out of the tank was there any reason to blow smoke at Stroud, telling him he had seen someone at Danish Landing who was carrying something that could have been a roll of wire and the guy didn't look anything like Verlyn? Verlyn was tall and thin, so Kit planned to say the guy he had seen was short and heavy. There was no point in getting mixed up with Stroud if it wasn't necessary. He wasn't entirely sure why he wanted to help Verlyn anyway beyond the fact that he would be entirely pissed, Kit the one who had saved him.

He retraced his steps through the woods and made his way to the garage. By the time he got inside the Toyota he had a new plan. For the time being he would forget Stroud. Instead, he'd find out what the deal was with Verlyn. He could hunt up Clappman and find out from him, but the quickest way was to check in with Mercy. She would know.

He would make one more stop after that, just to make sure of something. Then he would get the hell out of town.

NINETEEN

"NOTHING. ZERO. *Nada*."

"I get it," Fitzgerald said.

"Maybe the kid took a different road back," Calvin said. "There could be a lot of reasons."

"Where are you calling from?"

"The cabin. You want me to come over?"

"Better stay where you are. Maybe he'll show up there."

"Should I check with Jan?"

Fitzgerald didn't bother to relay the question to Mercy. He told Calvin not to call Jan under any circumstances and just wait in the cabin.

"Mercy and I will hunt around Ossning. We've got to figure Kit's still in trouble—that whoever killed Rawlings came to the campground intending to kill Kit. He meant to get rid of anyone who could connect him to Link's murder. If Kit shows up at your place, keep him there. It's too risky to take him back to Detroit now that somebody else knows the two of you were there."

"I sold the tickets," Calvin said. "Guy at the motel paid double."

"You earned it."

"Naw, the money's yours."

"We'll talk about it," Fitzgerald said. He was

about to hang up when Calvin asked him who else knew about Detroit.

"You told Jan, remember? And she called down."

"So what?"

"Think about it," Fitzgerald said.

"Think what?"

"She could be our killer. Maybe she knew Verlyn would be blamed for Link's death. With Verlyn out of the way she'd have the Kabin Kamp."

Calvin was quiet for a moment. Then he said, "Naw, that's too complicated. If she wanted Verlyn's place she'd kill him rather than Link."

"Women are complicated."

"Anyway, Jan wouldn't do it. Jan's a sweetheart."

Fitzgerald said, "Try telling that to Mercy."

LIGHTS HAD BEEN ON in Verlyn's and Jan's house, but Fitgerald's A-frame was pitch dark. Kit didn't get it.

If Verlyn was still in the tank, Mercy would be down at the jail, haranguing Stroud. Mercy and Verlyn were divorced, which meant she couldn't stand his guts anymore, yet she was always sticking up for him. She was always telling Kit to keep his shirt on as far as Verlyn was concerned and try to be more understanding. She kept reminding him Verlyn was his father, as if he could ever forget. Even in town he heard her defending Verlyn after he did something stupid and people were riled up.

But Verlyn wasn't in the tank. He was home tying flies. So why wasn't Mercy at the A-frame with
Fitzgerald?

That was where she was most of the time. Some
nights, the campground so cold and bleak he
wanted to put off going there as long as he could,
Kit drove to the A-frame and stopped out on the
road and looked up the driveway at the lights. He
wanted to knock at the door and go inside for a
while. Fitzgerald always had coffee going and the
smell mixed with that of the wood fire always going, too, and there were books everywhere and you
could sit in front of the fire, feet up on a big coffee
table after you pushed the books aside, and sense
through the glass front of the place behind you the
black woods leading down to the river.

Kit preferred Calvin's cabin as a place for a
guide to live, yet Fitzgerald's A-frame had its
points. If he ever won the goddamn lottery himself
he might get a place like it, temporarily, and just
for the hell of it. He figured it was the A-frame
Mercy went for and Fitzgerald was just part of the
deal.

But on those nights he never did knock at the
door and surprise them. Instead, he drove out to the
Keg O'Nails and hung out as long as the place
stayed open and took as much warmth as he could
store up back to the campground. He only went to
the A-frame when Mercy made a point of inviting
him to dinner and he could pretend he was doing
it to keep her happy. Fitzgerald told him to stop

anytime, and he showed him where he kept a key under a milk can on the back deck that was used as a flower planter. Kit said he didn't want to know, but he did, and now he was glad he did.

He was starving and figured he would make a couple peanut butter sandwiches to take with him in the Toyota. That way he could save his own dough, which was running low. But he had to move quick and hope Mercy and Fitzgerald didn't show up while he was inside. They liked to stop at the hotel after Mercy finished work and have a few drinks and listen to an old Finn play the accordion, and maybe that was where they were now.

He found the key with no trouble. What stopped him was the storm door—the glass busted out, some pieces still on the wooden steps. Why hadn't Fitzgerald or Mercy cleaned up after the accident? Both of them were neatness freaks as far as Kit was concerned.

The inner door wasn't locked and it looked like the lock had been busted. But when he switched on the kitchen light everything looked okay. There were two coffee mugs sitting on the trestle table along with a bottle of whiskey. For some reason, maybe because of the broken storm door and busted lock, he reached out and touched one of the mugs, acting like a TV detective.

The mug was still warm.

He experienced a bad moment, thinking he had walked in on Mercy and Fitzgerald in bed. That was the reason, the most obvious one, the A-frame was dark. But then he remembered neither Mercy's Suburban or Fitzgerald's Grand Cherokee were parked outside. It meant they couldn't be there, in bed. That fact, plus the warm mug, meant they had left the A-frame just a while before.

He took a swallow of whiskey from the bottle on the table, clamped his eyes shut until the stuff was down, then found bread and peanut butter in the cupboards and made himself two sandwiches. He was about to switch off the light and leave when the telephone rang in the living room. It froze him and he stood stock still, listening to the rings until the answering machine clicked on and he heard a voice asking something. He couldn't make out the question but the voice was distinct enough.

Calvin.

Kit went down the hallway from the kitchen and found a wall switch for an overhead light. He meant to play back the tape, hear what Calvin said. He had a pretty good idea what it was. Calvin was calling to tell Fitzgerald and Mercy that Kit had taken off from Detroit. But when the light came on he froze again.

The living room looked like a tornado had ripped through. The place was torn to pieces. His first thought was that Mercy and Fitzgerald had had a fight, tossing things at each other, but when he saw the tying table had been flipped over he knew that wasn't right. They wouldn't have done that.

When he looked in the bedroom Fitzgerald used as sort of an office he was certain it wasn't right.

The laptop computer was busted and so was Fitzgerald's Sage rod. He could imagine Mercy and
Fitzgerald pissed at each other enough to punch out
the storm door and even bust the computer, but they
wouldn't ruin a top-notch fly rod like that.

His impulse was to get out, and quick. Somebody
had broken into the A-frame and he didn't want to
be in the place when Fitzgerald and Mercy discovered it. Except they already had. They made coffee,
slugging it down with whiskey, then left. But why
do that? Why not call Willard Stroud and wait for
him to come out and see the mess?

He was in the kitchen and nearly out the door
when he remembered the telephone. He went back
into the living room and played the tape on the
answering machine. It was Calvin, all right. And
the question he was asking was clear.

So was the answer.

Calvin said, "I don't get it. What's Mercy got
against Jan?" Then he said, "I'm still at the cabin
waiting for the kid. Like you said."

KIT TOOK the bottle of whiskey with him when he
left the A-frame. Later on he would explain to Fitzgerald. Something told him that, given what was
going on, he would need the booze more than peanut butter sandwiches.

What exactly *was* going on?

He drove across Walther Bridge and at the South
Downriver Road turned in the direction of Ossning.
Along the way he munched on the sandwiches and

sipped the whiskey, the bottle stuffed between his thighs, and tried to think logically.

One: Verlyn was supposed to be in the tank but was home tying flies and watching the tube.

Two: Fitzgerald and Mercy ought to be in the A-frame but were gone and the place had been broken into and torn apart.

Three: Calvin had tickets for the ball game in Detroit but he was back at the cabin and on the phone asking about Jan.

Figure all that out.

But he couldn't—and, the more he thought about it, he realized it wasn't his business, anyway. His business had been with Stroud, but that was over, or over for the time being. So he was free to head back to Detroit—except that Calvin wasn't there anymore. He must have driven back to Ossning looking for him, ignoring the note Kit left for him. Sometimes Calvin was as dumb as Verlyn. And now he was calling up Fitzgerald and Mercy with a question about Jan.

To which Kit had the answer. That was one thing he had figured out.

When he reached Ossning he kept right on going, taking the highway through town and out toward Traverse City. The whiskey was making him light-headed but at the same time he was thinking better. From the start he had known what had happened, but now it all had a sharp edge to it. It was simple, plain, certain. Since he knew about Jan, it logically followed that he knew who killed Link Pickett.

He hadn't seen someone at Danish Landing, someone lugging something in the woods across the river. That was so much smoke he had blown in Calvin's direction. But he had seen Jan, all right— seen her somewhere else. And with someone other than Verlyn.

It was a hoot, when you thought about it. The fact that Jan was two-timing Verlyn would save Verlyn's ass, if it came to that. Maybe it wouldn't now that Verlyn was out of the tank. But it might. He might still have to see Stroud, telling him what he knew.

Pure pleasure welled up in Kit's mind, cutting through the warm haze of whiskey. He still had his old man right where he wanted him.

THE ORANGE neon sign of the Keg O'Nails glowed through the jack pines. Kit turned in and stopped a short distance from the front entrance of the restaurant and bar, keeping the Toyota running, giving himself just enough time to check the line-up of parked cars and trucks. He didn't expect to see what he was looking for here. As far as he knew they had never been dumb enough to park in front and let themselves be spotted inside the Keg O'Nails, and they sure wouldn't be dumb enough to begin now.

The parking lot extended back to the motel set tight against the pines. Lights coming from the place illuminated the area just in front, leaving the rest of the lot pitch black. Kit switched on his parking lights, the local custom when you ventured at night into the area behind the restaurant and bar, and began a slow tour of its outer edges.

You had to get close to a vehicle before you saw it, and you had only a brief sweep of your passing lights to make an identification. It was enough. He saw a couple vehicles he recognized—a Ford Econoline van, an old Buick stationwagon, a nearly rusted-out Plymouth Duster. He couldn't see anything of the couples inside, but he knew who they were. Not that he was interested.

What he was interested in he spotted halfway through his loop of the parking area. He had been certain it would be there, and it was—a big Chevy truck backed up against the pines, motor running like all the other vehicles in the lot. Kit took a quick look but kept on driving, making the slow loop, to all appearances just hunting for a vacant area to park himself. But by the time he came full circle back to the restaurant and bar he felt himself totally pissed off.

He didn't care if they had wiped out Link Pickett, both together or just one of them. Link and his stinking canoes were a menace to the river, so good riddance. Not that it made any difference. Somebody else would take over the business and rent out canoes and the river would continue going down the tubes. What was eating him was the fact that they had gotten away with it—and, the real point, knew they had.

They were out at the Keg O'Nails as if nothing

was different, no one the wiser. Right now they might be talking it over, telling themselves how all-shit smart they were.

Kit wasn't getting involved, not unless Stroud tried to pin Link's death on Verlyn. And he would only do that to put the needle in Verlyn. But one small thing would, right now, make him feel better. He wheeled the Toyota around, and as he did so he lifted the bottle and took another swallow of Fitzgerald's whiskey.

Making the loop of the parking area a second time he took a slightly different angle, so when he came up on the truck again he was heading almost directly toward it. He edged ahead until he was maybe twenty yards from it, then eased the brake down and at the same moment switched on his headlights and the overhead beam. The truck suddenly stood out in the darkness like a startled deer—shiny metallic gray, perfectly caught in the light. In the front seat two faces—stark white, features distinct—broke apart, then threw their hands in front of their eyes.

Kit gunned the car forward, turning sharply, rear tires spinning in crushed rock, firing stones outward like rifle shots. He raced across the parking lot and turned onto the highway without stopping, barreling back now toward Ossning, feeling again the smooth asphalt beneath him. He lifted Fitzgerald's whiskey to take another swallow and realized his hand was shaking so badly he couldn't locate his mouth.

He had gotten the whole thing wrong.

He meant to leave them sitting back there, thinking about it, figuring it was a wise-ass kid having fun. But the point was they would think about it. It would get something started in the back of their heads. A worry. A worry that maybe someone knew—and was letting them know he knew.

They had been picked out in the parking lot of the Keg O'Nails for a reason. It hadn't been a prank or an accident, and the more they thought about it the more they would worry.

But he had gotten it wrong.

He saw a pair of headlights in the rear view mirror. Overhead beams on. He watched until he was certain the vehicle was gaining on him. Then he slammed the accelerator to the floor and kept it there, cold sober now and scared.

TWENTY

THE FIRST PLACE Mercy and Fitzgerald thought of looking for Kit was at Danish Landing. But Kit told Calvin he was coming right back to Detroit, so he wouldn't have need of the campground—and Stroud probably had the entire landing closed off because of Rawlings' murder. Fitzgerald suggested they stop at the Kabin Kamp to see if Kit had been there and picked up his car, but Mercy didn't want to get Verlyn involved—and, for the time being, she didn't want Jan to know she and Fitzgerald were hunting for Kit.

So they took both vehicles into Ossning and made separate rounds of the town, trying to guess out where Kit might be. In the note he left for Calvin at the motel he said he was coming back to Ossning because he had something to do. But what? Until they knew that they didn't know where to begin looking for him.

Mercy checked the gas stations that were open twenty-four hours while Fitzgerald tried the fast-food places on the highway, the idea being that Kit might have picked up his car at the Kabin Kamp and gone into town for gas or food. Then Fitzgerald suggested looking in the bars and driving out to the Keg O'Nails, but Mercy said Kit wasn't old enough to drink. Even if he was he wouldn't have come back from Detroit just for that. Then Fitzgerald suggested girlfriends and Mercy said he wasn't old enough for them, either.

"He's nineteen," Fitzgerald said, and grinned at her. "Remember when you were?"

"Very funny," Mercy said.

They decided to leave the Suburban at Mercy's office and stay together in the Cherokee. One more circle through town took them past the hotel and then the Six-Grain Bakery, a CLOSED sign in the front window. The sign gave Mercy an idea.

"Let's assume Kit came back because of Link's death. Something about it. Calvin didn't know about Rawlings' death—he hadn't heard anything on TV or the radio—so Kit probably wouldn't have known, either. Link's death is the only one he knew about. And Kit said he saw someone at the landing, someone who in all likelihood was Link's killer, someone who wasn't Verlyn."

"Keep going," Fitzgerald said.

"So, given all that, there can only be one reason he came back. To tell who he saw out there. He came now because of what Jan told him on the phone."

"That Verlyn was in jail."

"He wasn't, of course, but Kit didn't know that. He didn't know Verlyn was already released. He only knew what Jan told him. That's got to be it."

"He wants to help Verlyn by telling Stroud what he saw."

"We didn't think to check for him at the city-county building."

"So let's do."

"Let's think first," Mercy said. "We agreed to bypass Stroud for the time being, work on our own. If we get mixed up with him now we'll have too much explaining to do. He'll have a stroke over all we've kept from him. So let's see if we can find out if Kit has seen him without asking Stroud himself. I know who'd know. And know about Laurel and Calvin, too."

"Bonnie Pym," Fitzgerald said.

Mercy said, "Bonnie knows everything."

SHE PHONED from the hotel, getting Bonnie out of bed. Mercy glanced at her watch and had a momentary sinking sensation. An entire generation, *her* generation, had descended into middle age. Bonnie Pym was in bed at nine o'clock!

"Sorry about the hour," Mercy said, "but I've got a favor to ask."

"Favor?"

"I'm in town with Fitzgerald. Would it be all right if we stopped over? It's urgent."

"Urgent?"

"It won't take long." There was silence on the other end of the line and Mercy had to say, "You still there, Bonnie?"

"I think so."

"So okay?"

"Okay, Mercy," a drowsy voice said.

Bonnie lived on the edge of Ossning in a manufactured house that had come to her in a divorce settlement—the second one, Mercy thought it was. The area was dark and the road in front unpaved and rutted, but lights were on in the house when Fitzgerald pulled up in front. Bonnie met Mercy at the door, wearing a robe, but with earrings and lipstick in place and exuding a cloud of perfume. Seeing her, Mercy felt a glimmer of hope. At least her generation wasn't going gentle into the good night.

"Fitzgerald's not coming in?" Bonnie asked. "There's beer in the fridge."

"I asked him to wait," Mercy said.

"Why?"

"So we can talk woman to woman."

Bonnie was clearly disappointed, but she led Mercy into the living room and halfheartedly offered her a beer.

"Not now. I want to make this quick, Bonnie. Was Kit in town today?"

"Was he supposed to be?"

"Look," Mercy said. "Kit may have come to town to tell Willard Stroud what he saw out at the campground. That's why I'm asking. He may be in trouble because of what he saw and I'm worried about him."

"No."

"No what?"

"He didn't come in to see Stroud. I'd have heard."

Mercy sighed. "That's good, I guess."

"But we close at five and I came home right away. He could have come to town later."

"I suppose."

"You're real worried, huh?"

"Worried enough." Then Mercy said there was something else she wanted to know. "It's about Laurel and Calvin. I've heard they were running around together before Link's death. Any truth to the story?"

"Plenty."

"And Link never knew?"

"You kidding? Laurel's still breathing. She wouldn't be, otherwise."

"But was it serious? I mean, would Laurel, now that Link was dead, want to marry Calvin? That serious?"

"You kidding?" Bonnie said again. "Calvin's in New Zealand half the time."

"She could go with him."

"She could but she wouldn't, not with that dream house she's got. And now the business. Anyway, she couldn't be without a man that long." When Mercy, suddenly looking closely at her, didn't respond, Bonnie looked back and said, "You said you wanted to talk woman to woman."

"I know I did."

"Well."

At the door Mercy signaled him and Fitzgerald got out of the Cherokee and came inside.

"Hey, sugar," Bonnie said to him. "Have a beer?"

Before he could answer, Mercy said, "Sit down and listen. I want you to hear what Bonnie just told me. It's about Calvin and Laurel."

"No big deal," Bonnie said. "They had something going together—a sort of a warm-weather thing. You know, while Calvin's around in summer. You get it?"

"I'm not sure," Fitzgerald said.

Mercy said, "Calvin's here only half the year. So what was Laurel doing the other half? Got it now?"

"She had a husband."

"If you want to be technical," Bonnie said. "The fact is Link was out of the picture long ago. Laurel kept him just happy enough to keep hanging around. It wasn't all that hard."

"You know that?" Fitzgerald asked.

"Don't ask how," Mercy said. "Bonnie knows."

"So who was her cold-weather friend?"

"Get a grip," Bonnie said. "Brand Pickett."

There was a long silence before Fitzgerald said to Bonnie, "I've got just one question. How do you know that?"

"About Laurel and Brand?"

"And Laurel and Calvin."

"Hey, sugar," Bonnie said, "I don't carry no tales. I seen them with these two eyes."

"Where?" Fitzgerald asked.

"Where the world goes round. Out at the Keg O'Nails."

BACK IN THE Cherokee Mercy said, "What do you think of that?"

"You tell me," Fitzgerald said.

"We're certain now who killed Link Pickett and Rawlings."

"Brand."

"And his sister-in-law."

"Laurel."

"Damn it all," Mercy said, "I got it wrong about Jan."

They talked it out, back and forth, while Fitzgerald drove around Ossning. What it came down to, or seemed to, was that Brand and Laurel had killed Link to clear the way so they could get married. It probably had something to do, too, with the canoe livery and the tackle shop, since with Link out of the way they would own the business completely. On the day of Link's funeral Laurel told Mercy that Brand had offered to buy her share of the business, but that must have been an attempt to divert attention away from what she and Brand really had in mind.

"Going around with Calvin," Mercy said, "that was probably more diversion. Laurel figured no one would guess she was interested in Brand if it got out that she and Calvin were a pair. And it was bound to get out. Maybe Laurel even figured that Link, learning about it, would go after Calvin and Calvin might come out on top. If Calvin killed Link then she and Brand wouldn't have to."

Fitzgerald said, "But they did. The opportunity

came when you told Laurel about the sting operation at Danish Landing. She told Brand and he
strung the wire across the river. When he and Laurel heard about Kit living in the campground Brand
went out there to silence him and ended up, after
he overheard my conversation with Rawlings, killing Rawlings.''

"Exactly.''

"But how do we know Brand was the one Laurel
really wanted? Maybe it was Calvin. Brand was the
diversion.''

"No way. Laurel wouldn't live in Calvin's cabin
and you'd never get him in her canopied bed.''

"You're sure?''

"Trust me. Laurel and Brand knew that suspicion would fall on Verlyn. They knew he'd strung
wire in the woods to ward off snowmobilers, and
they could guess that, Link dead, he'd boast he was
the one who'd killed him.''

"To help things along they went out of their way
to accuse Verlyn. Both of them raised a fuss with
Stroud.''

"And in Rawlings' case they knew Verlyn was
released from jail just earlier, so Brand used an arrow for the killing. That was something else that
could be associated with Verlyn.''

Fitzgerald said, "But they didn't plan on killing
Rawlings. We just said that. It was Kit they were
after. Did they think anyone would believe Verlyn
killed his own son?''

"I don't know. Maybe that's where they got out

on a limb. Once they knew Kit was in the campground, that he'd seen someone, they had to take a chance. Verlyn and Kit are always at each other. Everybody knows that. So maybe they reasoned people would think Verlyn was capable of doing it to keep Kit quiet. Lord, I don't know. Maybe when you're desperate you make yourself believe things like that."

"And Jan had nothing to do with it."

"It didn't mean anything when she called down to Detroit. She just wanted Kit to know about Verlyn."

"She was acting like a stepmother."

"Listen," Mercy said, "what I said before still goes."

"I remember. Under that safari suit—"

"Get your mind out of the gutter. We still don't have Kit."

Fitzgerald said, "There's one place we haven't checked."

"Well?"

"Calvin's."

They drove back to the hotel and Fitzgerald kept the Cherokee running while Mercy went inside to use the phone. The next thing he knew she was back and jerking the car door open.

"Talk to him."

"Calvin's on the phone?"

"*Please*. Just talk to him."

TWENTY-ONE

CALVIN SAID, "We got us another problem."

Then he began telling Fitzgerald what he had told Mercy. "All evening I'm tying flies and trying to stay awake in case Kit shows up here. Then I hear what sounds like his Toyota rattle to a stop outside. It's the kid, all right. In bad shape."

"He's there now?" Fitzgerald asked.

"That's what I'm saying."

"Great."

"Maybe not."

"After he settles down I learn what's gone on. Jan, when she called down to Detroit, told Kit that Stroud had Verlyn in jail. So Kit hitched back here to tell Stroud about seeing someone else out at Danish Landing. The idea was to get Verlyn off the hook, but it was nothing but smoke. He hadn't seen anything out there. He just wanted to pull one on Verlyn. He thought his old man would really be pissed off by that, Kit the one who'd saved him."

"Keep going," Fitzgerald said.

"So when he gets to town he goes out to the Kabin Kamp for his car and sees Verlyn there rather than in jail. It's a big disappointment. He's hitched all the way for nothing. The only thing to do is turn around, head back to Detroit, catch more of the Tigers.''

"Except he didn't."

"Because he's got another thing in his head besides pulling one on Verlyn. He's got the idea Jan's two-timing Verlyn by running around with Brand Pickett. So when he doesn't see Jan at the Kabin Kamp with Verlyn he figures she's out with Brand and decides to check to make sure.''

Fitzgerald said, "Where did he get that about Jan?"

"Where else? He saw them together. That's the thing. He didn't see anyone at the campground but he saw Jan and Brand loving it up at the Keg O'Nails.''

"Jesus," Fitzgerald said. "When?"

"Lots of times, he says.''

"Go on.''

"So he drives out and there they are in Brand's truck, just as he expects, and he decides to flash his headlights, dumb stuff, but he figures he'll feel better by making Jan realize somebody has her number. Somebody was telling her they knew she wasn't as worried about Verlyn as she made out. So what happens? He lights up the vehicle and there's Brand, all right. But it isn't Jan snuggling beside him.''

"And?''

"He has it screwed up. When Kit realizes this he takes off like a bat out of hell.''

"C'mon, Calvin. Who'd he see if it wasn't Jan?"

"Laurel." Calvin said it straight out, though it wasn't an easy thing to do. It was a bitter pill, actually. But facts were facts. "The kid's certain it was Laurel. I pushed him about it. He claims he isn't blowing smoke this time."

"You believe him?"

"Unfortunately."

"I know about it," Fitzgerald said.

"About Laurel and Brand?"

Calvin was going to ask him how he knew, but Fitzgerald wanted to know about Kit, about why he was at the cabin and in bad shape, so he went back to that.

"After Kit gets away from the Keg O'Nails he notices he's being followed and figures it has to be Brand and Laurel in the truck. He knows he can't outrun them in the piece of foreign junk he's driving, so he heads for my place, thinking maybe he can lose them when he turns in on the road through the pines. Then he can hole up here for a while."

Fitzgerald said, "And he knew you were there rather than in Detroit. How?"

"I'll tell you later," Calvin said. "The point is the kid's plenty happy I'm here. He knew he needed help when the headlights behind him on the highway didn't go past when he turned off. They followed him into the pines. Then they went dark."

"Meaning what?" Fitzgerald asked.

"Kit thinks Brand's waiting on the road into here. He knows there isn't another way out."

"But he assumes you're there."

"I've been thinking," Calvin said, "that's why he hasn't shown up yet. Why he's still out on the road. Brand's figuring what to do. He doesn't want to just come up and talk to Kit, ball him out for flashing his lights at him and Laurel, because that would get me involved. He'd as soon not do that."

"Because you've been running around with Laurel, too."

"You heard, huh?"

"But that's not it," Fitzgerald said. "Brand's thinking about something else."

"What?"

"We've got a big problem, Calvin. Brand and Laurel killed Link and Rawlings. I don't have time to explain, but Mercy and I are certain of it. So the first thing you've got to do is make sure the vehicle on the road is Brand's truck. Mercy and I will stick by the phone here at the hotel until you call back. And there's one other thing: Take a gun with you and make sure Kit has one, too."

"I don't believe in weapons," Calvin said.

"You don't have *any?*"

"I can take care of Brand without a gun," Calvin said, and hung up before Fitzgerald could object.

It took him longer to quiet Kit. "You got to stay put here," he told him. "You don't know the lay of the land along the road. You'd hold me up in the dark."

"Bullshit, Calvin."

"And somebody's got to stay by the phone."

"Bullshit."

"You know something?" Calvin said. "Verlyn's right about you. You're a pain in the rear."

AFTER HE slid out the cabin's door, the one opening on the river, Calvin quickly faded into the pines. The night was overcast but there was a faint sheen of moonlight coming through the clouds, enough to show the way along a needle-softened path that led out to the highway.

He had taken it several times on snowshoes when a wet early snow socked in the road and he couldn't get out in his pickup. From the path he could see the road a few feet off to his right, the dirt surface a pale silvery color against a black wall of trees. He could hear the soft slide of the river behind him, the sound fading as he moved forward.

He kept his eye on the road, hunting for the truck, and thought about who Kit said was in it. Brand and Laurel. Hearing that from the kid had been a shock, and having to tell Fitzgerald about it had been a turn of the screw. Yet the more he considered it the more it began to seem, beneath some bitterness he naturally felt at Laurel's two-timing, potentially good news.

If Laurel had something going with her brother-in-law that meant—didn't it?—that she wasn't overly serious about marriage. Maybe the marriage talk had never been serious, but just a way of shifting attention from what she had going with Brand. Maybe her whole relationship with Calvin had been nothing more than play acting, phony from the beginning.

That hurt—but only a little.

Calvin considered himself broadminded. He had Patty Dunvoold on the side, so it followed that Laurel could have something going with Brand Pickett. Fair was fair. There was, though, a difference. Patty Dunvoold was in New Zealand whereas Laurel was seeing him and Brand in Ossning at the very same time. No way could he square that.

But why, when you got right down to it, should he object? He could go on seeing Laurel through the summer—a widow now, so there was no need to sneak around Link—and let her talk all she wanted about marriage. Knowing he was sharing her with Brand was hard to take, but it wasn't enough of a pain to break off altogether. How many women as good looking as Laurel Pickett, and as available, were there in a place like Ossning?

Except—and the realization suddenly hit him hard—she might not be available for long. Not if Fitzgerald and Mercy were right. Not if Laurel and Brand had killed two people.

Then he saw something through the pines blocking the road that seemed another shade of black. He moved off the trail, angling to his left, circling away from the shape until he could come around to the road behind it. He crouched low, weaving through the straight shafts of the trees, making no sound. When he found the silvery track of the road again he eased himself through the trees and looked down it in the direction of the cabin.

There was the truck, the blocky shape filling the road, no lights on and the motor purring softly. It was too dark to see anyone inside, but that didn't matter. His mission had been to find the vehicle. The moment he saw it Calvin ducked back into the pines and retraced his steps to the cabin.

"GET OUT QUICK," Fitzgerald instructed him.

"Why?" Calvin said into the phone.

"Because it's too risky not to."

"But I don't get it. If Laurel and Brand are after the kid, why not come to the cabin? Why sit out in the truck?"

"You already answered that," Fitzgerald said. "It's because you're in the cabin, too. With you there they can't make up their minds. But it doesn't matter. They'll make a move sooner or later. As long as they believe Kit saw someone at the campground they'll have to act. They can't let Kit run free. That's why you've got to get out."

Calvin cradled the phone against his neck and pointed out what Fitzgerald already knew. "The only way out of the cabin is the dirt road and the truck has that blocked. I could take Kit out through the woods, circling around the truck, but what would we do once we reach the highway? Hitch a ride into Ossning?"

Fitzgerald said, "You could. But Laurel and Brand might guess you'd do that."

"So what else?"

"Jesus, Calvin. You tell me."

Calvin thought a minute, then took a look at Kit to see how he was dressed. The kid had enough clothes on to weather a night on Hudson Bay. "Paddle out," he said to Fitzgerald.

"What?"

"We'll get out one of my Old Towns, slip downriver, you can meet us as Schoolcraft Bridge. Simple as that."

"It's dark, Calvin."

"Not that bad."

For a moment Calvin could hear Fitzgerald talking with Mercy, their voices muted and speaking hurriedly. Then Fitzgerald was back on the phone.

"Mercy thinks it's a good idea."

"She's got good taste."

"She says it doesn't matter how dark it is. You know every inch of the South Branch. You can canoe it blindfolded."

"I didn't want to say so myself," Calvin said.

"Leave all the lights on in the cabin. Make it look like you're still there. Turn the TV on."

"I only watch ball games on the tube."

"So?"

"There isn't one tonight."

"Brand and Laurel don't know that."

"Yeah," Calvin said, "but you got to think of your reputation."

Fitzgerald said, "C'mon, Calvin. Get cracking."

"I'm gone," Calvin said.

KIT GAVE HIM static. Kids that age wouldn't do anything because you told them to. They had to have reasons, and reasons took time, and even when they had the reasons they still gave you static. He could understand why Verlyn was usually sick to death of the kid.

"Move!" Calvin had to tell him.

While he and Kit got one of the Old Towns out of the garage beside the cabin Calvin explained everything he knew—about Laurel and Brand, about Mercy and Fitzgerald thinking the two of them were responsible for the killings, about the fact Kit was in danger because of what he had seen from the campground at Danish Landing.

"Yeah," Kit protested, "but I made that up."

"It doesn't matter. You said you saw someone. Laurel and Brand, they couldn't let you go telling that to Willard Stroud."

"So?"

"So they meant to wipe you out. That's why we went down to the ball games in Detroit. To keep you from getting wiped out."

Kit dropped his end of the canoe. "You shouldn't have lied to me! You should have told me the real reason for going to Detroit."

"You would have gone then?"

"Hell, no."

"You know something?" Calvin said. "You don't pick up that canoe I'll bash you myself."

Kit turned sullen after that, but he kept moving. They lowered the canoe into water on the edge of the river and Kit held it steady while Calvin went back to the garage for a pair of paddles. Seeing the lights on in the cabin and hearing the TV, he felt a stab of pain for the waste of energy. It wasn't the money involved, but the principle. If the lights and the sound kept Laurel and Brand out there on the road a while longer, puzzling over what to do about Kit, maybe it was worth it. But it stung him nonetheless.

He got Kit settled in the front of the canoe, then put one foot in the rear and pushed off with the other. The canoe scraped the river bottom, then eased through flat water before meeting the current and turning hard downstream. Ahead of him Kit held his paddle across the gunwales, arms braced against it, and looked around.

"Keep your eyes ahead," Calvin told him. "Watch for sweepers."

"You haven't been on the river before?"

"Not since I got back. I don't know what we're in for."

"Terrific."

"I'll handle the canoe. Keep your paddle dry unless you see something ahead. Water high like this, we don't have extra time for corrections if there's a problem."

"You think I'm some kind of Indian?" Kit said over his shoulder. "I can't see a damn thing."

"Your eyes will adjust. It's never completely dark on the river. You can always see enough to pick out a route."

"Bullshit, Calvin."

"There's something I forgot to say," Calvin said. "Keep your eyes ahead and your mouth shut."

THE NIGHT WAS colder than Calvin had anticipated. He had a down vest over a thick turtleneck and a wool shirt but the cold still bothered him. He felt it most around the head. He should have put on a wool watch cap, pulling it down over his ears, rather than his fishing stetson.

The downside of spending the off season in New Zealand was it changed your metabolism in some way and you weren't set up any longer, biologically speaking, for Michigan weather, which was usually a version of winter except for a hot and humid stretch that came in August. Even August could be a version of winter. Before he had the cabin and spent summers camping on a piece of Verlyn's property, he now and then had to thaw water in August for his morning coffee.

Ahead of him Kit was hunched over, parka hood drawn over his head. He had spotted a couple downed cedars, which meant his eyes had adjusted, but Calvin had already seen them and maneuvered around. They were shooting ahead on the current, making the turns with sharp cuts, covering water. Calvin had been able to pick up the dim shape of landmarks and had a good idea where they were.

There was nothing to worry about. Fitzgerald and Mercy would be waiting at Schoolcraft Bridge, they would get the canoe out of the water and tied down on top of whatever vehicle they had brought, then fire off into Ossning. Fitzgerald had said they would head straight to Stroud's office and tell him everything they knew and see that Kit was given protective custody. There was nothing to worry about.

Except one thing.

It wasn't, Calvin realized, only the cold that was bothering him. For several minutes now he had felt the presence of another canoe on the river. It was something a guide could always sense. When you were working it was only an irritation, another fishing party behind you, pushing you, breaking into your concentration. But this was another matter.

He knew what had happened. It had been dumb, not thinking about the possibility earlier, not doing something about it then. Now it was too late.

"Wet your paddle," he called out to Kit. "Now!"

TWENTY-TWO

FROM THE MAIN DRAG of Ossning it was twelve miles to Schoolcraft Bridge on the South Branch of the Borchard. But Mercy insisted they couldn't go until they both were armed. They couldn't take the gamble. The double-barrel shotgun was still in the Cherokee, along with Fitzgerald's camping gear, but her service revolver had been returned to the locked container in the Suburban. So they delayed long enough to drive from the hotel to Mercy's office.

On the drive to Schoolcraft Bridge Fitzgerald gripped the steering wheel with both hands and pumped the accelerator to the floor.

"We lost time. That could be important."

Mercy said, "Don't tell me what I know. At least we'll be able to put up a fight."

"If that happens."

On the west side of the bridge there was a turn into a narrow dirt road that ran for fifty yards to a small crushed-stone parking area and canoe landing. Pines had been cleared back and logs placed end to end at the edge of the river to protect the bank from erosion. At the bridge a single halogen light sent an orange glow through the pines and onto the canoe landing. Fitzgerald stopped the

Cherokee a few feet from the bank, facing the river, headlights on so Calvin and Kit could see where to bring the canoe in.

"We might have missed them," Mercy said. "They might have gone past."

Fitzgerald asked her how long it took to paddle from Calvin's cabin to the bridge, and when Mercy told him an hour at best he said they couldn't have missed them. "Besides, Calvin wouldn't go past the landing. He knows the river too well. You said so yourself."

"I know what I said."

"And he knows how long it takes to reach the next landing."

Mercy said, "That's the long stretch—no roads or bridges through the Overmeyer Tract."

"So how much canoe time?"

"Six hours. Five if you push it."

"So we just wait here," Fitzgerald said. "He won't miss this landing."

"I know."

"Then relax."

Mercy leaned back against the car seat, then instantly popped forward. "Let's wait outside. Maybe we'll hear them coming."

"Not the way Calvin paddles."

"Damn it," Mercy said, "don't be so wise."

Fitzgerald shrugged and reached for the door.

"And bring the shotgun."

PADDLING, Kit didn't see the sweeper until it was on top of the canoe. "Get down!" Calvin shouted at him, and in the same instant swung the canoe hard to the left, nearly spinning it in the water. It was too late. The branches of the cedar came across the bow, catching Kit squarely, just as the canoe dipped sharply to the side. Kit grasped for one of the gunwales but his balance was gone, his weight tipped too far, and he toppled into the water.

Calvin reached out and got hold of a limb, steadying the canoe, forcing it sideways against the cedar. Bare limbs whipped him across the face. With his other hand he jammed the paddle inside the canoe and grasped his stetson, keeping it from being swept into the water along with Kit. He could hear water breaking against the downed tree, a concentrated sound like white-water rapids, and at the same time hear Kit's padded arms flailing the surface.

"Get hold of the canoe!" he shouted at him. "Straighten up!"

Easier said than done. He had gone in like Kit plenty of times, feet swept out from under him and held horizontally in the current, body encased in a cocoon of clothing that seemed to make him as buoyant as a float tube, carried helplessly downstream even though the river depth was no more than three feet or so.

"Work at it!" he shouted again. "Get your feet down!"

If he went in himself to help the kid he might overturn the canoe—both of them soaked then and wasting time getting the canoe onto the bank, getting back in, getting started again. It was time they didn't have. He heard Kit spitting water and trying to talk, then saw him upright at the bow, a hand on the gunwale and another on a limb, balanced now between the canoe and the downed cedar.

"You've got it!" Calvin called to him. "Hold the canoe, we'll work it back along the sweeper. Keep your footing. Grab a branch before you take a step."

He pulled off the stetson, got it safely inside the canoe, then reached out for another limb and pulled the canoe after him, letting the branches snap across his face, forcing the canoe toward the bank. The current eased as they got farther in and he could see Kit for the first time, a dark shape leaning over the gunwale, one arm extended into the cedar.

"You're okay," Calvin called to him. "You're moving."

Kit mumbled something but Calvin couldn't make out what it was.

"When you get out of the water," Calvin said, "you're going to think you're freezing to death. You're not. It just feels that way."

MERCY SAID, "It's darker than I thought."

"Sure," Fitzgerald explained. "The car lights like this, aimed across the river into the pines, they exaggerate the speed of the current. And they exaggerate the darkness outside the light. For Calvin and Kit it won't seem so black. Out there they won't have the contrast with light and dark.''

"That's encouraging," Mercy said. "Is it true?"

Fitzgerald was about to go into more detail, making it up on the spot, anything to ease the anxiety Mercy felt and he felt as well, when they both heard a vehicle cross the bridge and turn onto the canoe-landing road. They watched as the vehicle came toward them, moving slowly, low beams on, and stopped beside the Cherokee.

"Maybe Stroud," Mercy said.

Fitzgerald was about to tell her he didn't think so, that Willard Stroud had no way of knowing they were at Schoolcraft Bridge, when the headlights switched to high beams and they were blinded in a brilliant burst of blue-white light.

Mercy crouched, shielding her eyes, pulling the service revolver from her parka pocket while Fitzgerald extended the shotgun, holding it against his hip, trying to direct the barrels toward the center of light.

"I wouldn't," Laurel Pickett told them.

"LIKE HELL," Kit said when Calvin told him again he was all right. "I *am* freezing to death."

Calvin held the canoe against the bank and crawled out onto spongy ground and a tangle of tree roots. They were on the other side of the sweeper now and as far as he could tell the river ahead looked clear. Kit stayed behind in water to his knees, motionless, arms rigid. Calvin couldn't see his face but he knew the expression that would be on it.

"You're cold," he told him. "There's a difference. The water's forty-six degrees. I checked the other day on the mainstream. You start moving you'll feel okay. You got to get the blood pumping."

"This goddamn river sucks."

"We got dumped. That happens."

"*I* got dumped."

Calvin didn't have time to argue with the kid—or explain about the mistake he had made. When Laurel and Brand had finally come up to the cabin, discovering the two of them gone, it wouldn't have taken much figuring to know what had happened. He and Kit couldn't have taken the road out. Going through the woods was a possibility, but it would have been a tough walk.

Taking the river made the most sense, and when Laurel and Brand found one of the Old Towns missing in the garage they knew exactly what had happened. Laurel knew he kept two canoes for guiding, and Brand probably knew, too. But that wasn't his mistake, leaving a canoe behind for Laurel and Brand to find, though it would have been smart if he and Kit had at least hidden it in the woods.

The mistake was not realizing they would figure out the route, too—that he and the kid would head for the landing at Schoolcraft Bridge. Brand knew the river best, so he would follow them with the

canoe while Laurel drove to the landing to head
them off there. Calvin had never thought about Laurel and Brand splitting up. It was a military tactic
he had read about. A pincer movement.

Now, Kit dumped in the water, they had wasted
time. Brand, digging hard in the river, could be
right behind them, probably armed and slipping
through the darkness before they could spot him.
Even if they stayed ahead, both he and Kit digging
hard, they would run into Laurel covering the landing. The river was narrow at the bridge. There was
no way they could shoot past if Laurel was paying
attention.

"Come on," he said, and reached out for Kit,
getting his arm and hauling him up on the bank. "I
got an idea."

"Goddamn terrific," Kit said. "I'm freezing,
you've got an idea."

"Listen," Calvin told him. "There's no time to
argue. Here's the deal."

He gave the kid a quick rundown of the situation.
"Brand's behind us in the other Old Town, Laurel's
at Schoolcraft Bridge, and both of them are probably armed. We're in trouble and maybe Mercy and
Fitzgerald, too. So we've got to get rid of one of
our problems, which is where the sweeper comes
in. Your getting dumped in the river was a blessing
in disguise."

Kit said, "You're losing it, Calvin. You know
that?"

"Just *listen*. The downed cedar, it narrows the

river to six feet or so. When he spots it Brand will have to slow the canoe so he can work through the channel. We wait in the water, using the branches of the cedar for cover.''

''Then what?''

''When he slows the canoe I'll step out from the cover and deck him with a paddle. At the same time you grab the gunwale of his canoe with both hands and push down. Give it all your weight. You dump him and any weapons he has in the river.''

''Then what?''

''When Brand's in the water you push his canoe past the cedar, let the current shoot it downstream. After that we get to the bank on the other side of the sweeper. We get back in our canoe and have clear sailing to the bridge.''

''Yeah,'' Kit said, ''but what if Brand spots us before we spot him?''

''He won't. We'll be covered in the cedar and he'll be concentrating on getting past. It'll work.''

''So we get to the landing and there's Laurel.''

''We'll pull in before we get there. Go overland through the woods. Laurel won't figure us coming that way. We'll have the advantage of surprise.''

''And maybe she's armed to the teeth.'' Then Kit said, ''Your idea means you get wet, too.''

''I thought of that.''

''You'll think you're freezing,'' Kit said, and suddenly grinned at him, ''but you're only cold.''

''PUT WHAT YOU GOT on the ground there,'' Laurel said. ''Slow like.''

Beside him Fitzgerald felt Mercy hesitate. But the two guns were useless when neither of them could see a target. "Do it," he told her sternly. Then he bent at the knees, eyes squeezed shut against the flame of blue-white light, and eased the shotgun to the ground.

He hadn't heard the doors of the vehicle open but from the sound of Laurel's voice she had to be outside it, just off to the side, facing them. But where was Brand? Was he beside her, back behind the light, the one covering them?

"Okay," he said when Mercy placed the service revolver on the ground, "now cut the lights."

Laurel ignored him. "Turn yourselves around and face the river. Slow like."

"Damn it, Laurel," Mercy said. "What's going on?"

The sound was sharp, distinct, metallic. When Fitzgerald heard it he crouched involuntarily as if he expected a blow to the stomach. Beside him, Mercy didn't seem to move a muscle. The sound of the hammer being snapped back had come from the direction of the voice, but it might be Brand out there with a shotgun. Or Laurel. Or both of them together.

"Do it," he said to Mercy, and slowly turned his back into the lights.

Now, the headlights of two vehicles on it, the far bank of the river had the appearance of a movie screen, the light concentrated on glistening water and a blank wall of pine, impenetrable black night on both wings. He felt even more helpless than he had before. With his back to the lights he could see now—but see what? He glanced at Mercy and their eyes met, held for an instant. Behind them was the sound of footsteps on the crushed stone, Laurel moving closer. Or Brand.

"That's it?" Mercy said. "That's the plan? You're going to shoot us in the back?"

Laurel said, "Now Mercy."

Fitzgerald thought Mercy was going to swing around, confront Laurel. He glanced at her again, trying to catch her eye, imploring her to keep her back to the lights.

"*Now Mercy?*" she said. "What the hell is this, Laurel? We don't even get an explanation?"

He let his breath out slowly, relaxing almost. Mercy was under control. She was trying to buy time, get Laurel talking, giving them time to think. But think about what? If he and Mercy made a break at the same time into the opposite wings of darkness Laurel might hit only one of them. If they were lucky. But if Brand was back there, both of them armed, even luck wouldn't be enough. They would never make it.

Laurel said, "I tried to get you to stay away."

"By telling me you were going around with Calvin? By all that nonsense about marrying him? Is that what you mean? Or do you mean the A-frame, too—trashing it that way?"

"We both tried to tell you."

"Tell me what, Laurel?"

"To leave us alone."

"You and Brand? Is that what this is all about? Laurel, we don't care about you and Brand. Do what you damn well want with Brand. Marry him if you want. We're here for Kit."

Laurel sighed audibly before she said, "So am I, Mercy."

THE SOUTH BRANCH usually ran warmer than the mainstream of the Borchard, but this time of year you couldn't tell and a couple degrees didn't matter anyway when you were nearly freezing to death. Calvin was in water up to his hips, pushed back into the branches of the cedar, nearly fastened there by the power of the current. He gripped a paddle with both hands and dug his boots into the stone bottom of the river, ready to push off and force himself across the current.

He could just see Kit off to the side and slightly ahead of him, a dim shape against the branches of the cedar. He had told the kid to make sure of his footing so he could lunge ahead when the time came and grab the canoe just after Calvin went for Brand. Waiting in the river was the miserable part but there was no way around it. If they waited on the shore until they spotted the canoe it would be too late.

Then it happened.

Calvin saw nothing, but he heard the sound—a paddle scraping the side of the canoe. Then he heard it again, closer now.

Brand was getting sloppy, thrashing the river, trying to make time. He would put on the brakes hard when he spotted the sweeper, all his attention on it, never figuring on two dark shapes springing out of the branches. Calvin smiled into the black night.

The sonofabitch might die of surprise before he felt the blade of the paddle.

TWENTY-THREE

FITZGERALD GLANCED at her, saw a shadowed face rigid with anger. Mercy knew now. She knew all he knew.

Laurel and Brand had figured out that Kit was on the river with Calvin, that the two of them had taken a canoe from the cabin and were heading to Schoolcraft Bridge, that she and Fitzgerald were at the landing to meet them. When Kit showed up in the canoe, Laurel and Brand would force him in the truck. They likely would shoot out the tires of the Cherokee first so they couldn't be followed.

That was one possibility.

Another was Kit wouldn't live long enough to get inside the truck. That meant he and Mercy and Calvin had no future, either. But Laurel and Brand would have to be crazy to do that.

Were they?

Mercy kept Laurel talking, explaining herself, trying to get Mercy to understand. Laurel said, "Kit shouldn't have been staying in the campground. It was nearly winter still. You shouldn't have allowed it, Mercy."

"I didn't."

"But he was there anyway. He saw the two of them in the woods across the river. It was just where you said Link would be arrested for cutting a sweeper. That was the start of everything.''

"Wait a minute," Mercy said. "You said *them*. Don't you mean you and Brand? You two strung the wire.''

"No, Mercy. ''

"Who then?''

"Link and Brand.''

"What?''

"No one killed Link.''

"What?''

"When I told Link what you said he got an idea that would put Verlyn in hot water. He knew about Verlyn's trouble with the sheriff for using wire in the woods, so Link got the same kind of wire and strung it across the river at Danish Landing. Brand helped him. He was going to pretend he just noticed it when he got there, then drop down in the canoe and slide under at the last moment. He'd have witnesses—you and your boss—that the wire was there and would have killed him otherwise.''

"Good Lord.''

"But something went wrong. I don't know what. Maybe Link forgot exactly where he'd strung the wire. Maybe, with the river high and strong that day, he came on the wire faster than he meant and couldn't get down in the canoe in time. No one will ever know for certain. Link is dead and he did it himself. He committed suicide.''

"Suicide?''

"Yes.''

"But it was an *accident,* Laurel."

"Not with Link and Brand putting up the wire, it isn't. Everybody will think they did something dumb and then fouled it up and Link got himself killed. He'd pulled a dirty trick and it backfired. Killing himself that way was worse than regular suicide. Everyone in town will talk about how that dumb Link Pickett ended up killing himself on the river. They'll never forget. And I'll always be remembered as his wife and Brand as his brother."

"Good Lord."

"So after it was over and nothing could be done, Brand and I wanted the sheriff to think Verlyn had killed Link. We wanted everybody to think that. We were free now to get married, but we decided to go slow. We don't want anyone getting the idea Brand might have killed Link because of me."

Mercy said, "So you told me about Calvin. You were trying to keep attention off Brand."

"Calvin was just something to do in summer when Link and Brand were busy at the livery. A way of filling up the time. Brand was the same. He fooled around some with Jan but it didn't mean a thing. Brand loves me and I love him."

"It must have looked like you were home free," Mercy said. "Everyone thinks Verlyn is the killer; he even went around bragging he was. Then it began falling apart: you learned about Kit."

Laurel said, "If Kit said he saw Link and Brand in the woods, the real story of the suicide could come out. So Brand went out there to the campground. He wanted to find out for sure what Kit had seen. He wanted to have a talk with him.''

''And he just happened to have a hunting bow with him?''

''We couldn't let Kit go to the sheriff. Don't you understand?''

Mercy said, ''Goddamn it, Laurel. Brand went out there to kill my son. That's what I understand. Then he ran into Rawlings and switched plans and killed him instead. Or were you with him? Did Brand kill Rawlings or did you?''

''Brand didn't want to. He didn't even know Rawlings. But he wouldn't leave us alone. He was just like you, Mercy. All of you were on Verlyn's side.''

''Because he didn't *do* anything. Good Lord, Laurel, listen to yourself. Brand killed Rawlings to cover up an *accident*. That's all it was. Now you've got us out here with a gun in our backs. Look what's happened.''

Laurel said nothing and they could hear her scraping the crushed stone with a boot. When she finally spoke there was an edge of sadness in her voice. ''I guess it's like love, Mercy.''

''Love?''

''Once you start in there's no stopping.''

BRAND WASN'T THERE.

Fitzgerald was almost certain of it now. Brand wouldn't let Laurel go on like that, let Mercy keep her talking. He would break in, take charge.

But where was he?

Kit had seen Laurel and Brand together in Brand's truck at the Keg O'Nails and Calvin had seen the truck on the cabin road. A big vehicle like that had pulled up to the canoe landing and frozen Mercy and him with high beams. Brand could be back there, waiting inside the truck.

But that didn't make sense. He wouldn't let Laurel handle the situation alone. Not someone like Brand Pickett.

So where was he?

When it came to him the answer hit Fitzgerald like a blow, sucking out his breath. Brand and Laurel must have gotten out of the truck at the same time. While she covered Mercy and him, Brand must have circled around the headlights to the edge of the river. He must be waiting there in the dark for Calvin and Kit. When they paddled into the headlights, thinking it was Fitzgerald's Cherokee lighting the landing, they would be sitting ducks.

He hadn't heard any footsteps on the crushed rock other than Laurel's, but that didn't mean anything. He'd been protecting his eyes from the high beams of the truck, concentrating on that. He hadn't been listening carefully. If Laurel had any trouble, Brand could get involved. Otherwise he was the hit man, waiting for Calvin to bring Kit to him, perfectly centered in beams of blue-white light.

And afterward?

He had wondered if Laurel and Brand were crazy

enough to kill everyone. Now Laurel had answered the question.

Once you start in, love or killing, there is no end to it.

TWENTY-FOUR

MERCY SAID, "I detect a rather large problem, Laurel. Won't Willard Stroud find it strange, a bunch of dead bodies on the South Branch? What's he supposed to think? Verlyn killed us all?"

"Now Mercy."

"Well?"

"We just want to talk to Kit. He's just going with us a while, is all. Nobody's getting killed, Mercy. We're just waiting here for Kit."

"You're letting us go when you get Kit? Is that what you're saying?"

"I said we're just waiting for Kit."

"But think about it. If you let us go we'll tell everything you said and there goes your story about Link."

"It's just your word, Mercy. Brand and I won't know what you're talking about. Nobody will believe you."

"Want to bet?"

"Now Mercy. Kit's the only one who matters. He was the one in the campground."

FITZGERALD TRIED to catch Mercy's attention. She was careful not to move her head but her eyes shifted, met his. They were connected.

Planning.

They couldn't trust Laurel. They both knew that. Brand might hit Kit with an arrow the moment the canoe entered the headlights beamed across the river. Or maybe he would use a gun this time. Even if Laurel was telling the truth they couldn't take the chance. If Laurel held the two of them at gunpoint while Brand got Kit in the truck, what would happen then?

The odds were Kit would end up like Rawlings, his body dumped somewhere in the jack pines. They both knew that, too.

Fitzgerald shifted his eyes from one side to the other. When Mercy frowned in response he did it again, exaggerating his eye movement. This time she blinked her eyes, doing it slowly, signaling back.

At the same moment they would break in opposite directions, both diving for the darkness beyond the tunnel of light. If she was going to fire, Laurel would have to choose one of them before the other was swallowed up in the night. If she had time to consider, Fitzgerald calculated, she would choose him. She would rather have another woman loose in the darkness than a man.

Would Laurel really think that way?

He offered a rapid prayer she would.

"AND WHAT HAPPENS to Kit after this talk with you and Link?"

"Now Mercy."

"You know something, Laurel? You say that again and I'm going to turn around and make you use that gun."

"I wouldn't do that."

"All right. Don't get excited. Just answer the question. Tell me what happens to Kit."

"We'll have to see."

"That's no answer." Then Mercy said, "Now listen. This is important, Laurel. Kit didn't see anything in the campground. He wanted to protect Verlyn, that's all. He made up the story. You hear me? He was camping at Danish Landing but he didn't *see* anything from the high banks. I swear, that's the truth."

"Everybody says he did."

"That's our fault. Fitzgerald and I planted the story around town. We were trying to help Verlyn and hoped the story would bring out the real killer. But that doesn't matter, Laurel. I'm telling you, Kit didn't see anything out there."

"You'd say that, wouldn't you?"

"Because it's *true*."

"Now Mercy."

IT WAS NOW or never. He couldn't be certain how long Mercy could hold together, going back and forth with Laurel, buying time. And for what?

He got her eye again, signaled again, and Mercy responded. Then he opened and closed his mouth three times, and when Mercy frowned he did it again, exaggerating the movement of his lips. This time she blinked her eyes in response. She had it. God help him, he hoped she did.

At the count of three they would break for darkness.

Mercy was talking again, trying to keep Laurel's attention, but Fitzgerald didn't listen. He thought again about Brand, about where he might be positioned. Was Mercy wondering, too? But you couldn't figure everything. Sometimes you had to trust to luck. It raced through his head that he had won the Michigan lottery once, that he had found someone he wanted to marry, that he might have used up all the luck a man could reasonably expect in this world.

Then he opened his mouth, beginning the count. Mercy was watching him.

One, two—

At three he plunged hard to his left, boots slipping as they dug through loose rock, making for black night. He had taken two or maybe three steps, halfway there, when the shotgun went off and the light coming from the headlights turned a hellish orange. His legs flashed warm, then turned into an undifferentiated mass of searing heat.

He knew he was hit and it came to him as immense relief.

Laurel had chosen him.

He stayed on his feet until he reached blackness, then fell, drawing into himself so that he tumbled, rolling ahead. He was beyond crushed rock now, into scrawny grass. He crawled through it, pushing himself with his arms, knowing the woods began just beyond. Both legs seemed useless, but his arms and shoulders were all right. He had seen animals hit by cars, their hindquarters useless, yet dragging themselves ahead with forelegs.

The image flicked through his mind. He was making it, a wounded animal.

Then the shotgun went off again, three rapid blasts. He felt no more pain, only his legs burning up on him now, so he hadn't been hit again. Laurel was firing wildly in his direction, or was she firing at Mercy? Or was it Brand? Was he firing, too?

He could tell nothing about the direction the shots had come from.

He kept forcing himself ahead, reaching the trees, getting inside the black shelter of them, feeling safe then but worrying about Mercy. If she was okay, hidden in the woods on the other side of the landing, the shots might alert Calvin and Kit. They would turn the canoe into the bank. They wouldn't keep heading into the ambush at Schoolcraft Bridge.

He grasped a pine, trying to pull himself up, but the branches wouldn't hold and he slipped back down, the bark ripping skin from his face. He rolled to the side, found a larger tree, worked himself up into the branches so that he was standing, balanced against the tree. He extended a hand down one leg, feeling the length of pain, his fingers edging through a hot ooze of blood.

The sound of voices came to him then, shouting

back and forth, a man's voice dominating. Then a woman's protest rang out, the voice clear and distinct and familiar, and the pain seemed to slip from him. He tried to move on his shattered legs, heading toward the voices.

"Damn you, Calvin!" he heard Laurel Pickett say again. "Let me up!"

"DON'T LET her move," Mercy commanded. "Break her back if you want."

Laurel was face down on crushed stone, Calvin crouched over her, a knee pressed into her back. Kit stood beside him, gripping Laurel's shotgun. Mercy looked down long enough to be satisfied, then wheeled away, searching beyond the blue-white light, calling out Fitzgerald's name.

When she heard an answering call she ran from the light, stumbling in her haste. She found him crumpled at the base of a tree, holding a torn limb in one hand. She touched his face, found blood there, then followed his other hand down his leg. As Fitzgerald twisted away from her touch she shouted back in the direction of the light.

"Kit! Help me!"

TWENTY-FIVE

"BRAND?" FITZGERALD MANAGED to ask on the way to the hospital.

"It's okay," Mercy told him. She and Kit had gotten him stretched out on the back seat of the Cherokee. She was squeezed onto the floor beside him, cradling his head while Kit drove.

"Laurel?"

"Calvin's in charge of her. It's okay, too."

"How?"

"Calvin and Kit—they did it. Don't talk now. Just try to relax. It's all okay."

Mercy stayed in the emergency room waiting area while Kit and Calvin took Laurel to Willard Stroud's office in the city-county building. Finally the young doctor on duty came out and told her Fitzgerald was a lucky man. Although the shotgun had been fired at close range, he hadn't taken the full force of the blast.

"We still have pellets to dig out. And he's lost blood."

"That's all?"

"It's enough."

"I mean—"

"Will there be permanent damage? I wouldn't expect so."

Later the doctor came out again and told her Fitzgerald was being moved to a hospital bed. He would have to remain for three or four days. "He wants you to bring him a book. He said you would know which one."

"I do."

"'Whether we live by the sea-side, or by the lakes and rivers, or on the prairie, it concerns us to attend to the nature of fishes.' He quoted something like that."

"That's him, all right."

"You know what it means?"

"Haven't the faintest."

She wanted to spend the night at the hospital but the doctor told her there was no need, and when Stroud sent a patrol car for her she left for the city-county building. She saw Gus Thayer of the *Call* in the hallway but went past him without saying anything. Kit and Calvin were in Stroud's office, in dry clothes now, sipping coffee and munching on what looked like stale sweet rolls.

"Black coffee," she told Stroud, "and no lectures."

"Coffee, anyway," Stroud said, and handed her a steaming styrofoam cup. Then he said, "Well?"

"Fitzgerald's lucky to be alive."

"I knew he was lucky. I didn't know he was as ornery as you."

"He saved our lives," Mercy said. "Laurel would have killed us."

"I didn't mean that. I meant the two of you sticking your noses in the case. You got in my way, Mercy.''

''That's one way of looking at it. Another is we did your job for you.''

Stroud waited, sipping his coffee, eyeing her closely. Then he said, ''Fitzgerald planning to write anything for his paper?''

''He's in the hospital, Stroud.''

''When he gets out.''

''That depends.''

''On what?''

''On whether you say one more goddamn word.''

SHE AND KIT and Calvin gave their statements, and after they signed the printouts the three of them walked down the main drag to the hotel. Mercy said she needed something to drink after Stroud's coffee. And she wasn't ready yet to drive back to the A-frame and face the mess there.

''They smashed up Fitzgerald's rod,'' Kit said.

''How do you know that?''

''I stopped at your place after I got my car. Before I went out to the Keg O'Nails, then Calvin's place.''

Calvin said, ''That's how Kit knew I wasn't still down there in Detroit. I left a message on your answering machine. He played it back.''

''Thank God.''

''Fitzgerald's probably wondering,'' Calvin said. ''I told him I'd tell him how Kit figured out I was at the cabin.''

"We'll clear it up later," Mercy said.

"There something you should know," Kit said. "While I was at your place I made a couple peanut butter sandwiches."

"Good."

"And took the jug of whiskey on the table."

Mercy stared at him. Then she sighed and said, "We'll clear that up later, too."

At the bar Calvin got an O'Doul's for himself from Sandy and schooners of real beer for Kit and Mercy. Mercy wanted to protest that Kit wasn't old enough, but it was a little late for that and she was too tired. She eased herself onto one of the padded bar stools beside her son. In the morning, she knew, she wouldn't want to believe she had done that— nor think about what Kit had done with the whiskey.

The only other patrons of the bar were Nils and Wilma. Nils' stint with the accordion was finished, the dining room beyond the bar empty and the overhead lights turned low, but he and Wilma were not ready to head into the night. Watching them at the end of the bar, seeing the two old figures speaking softly to one another, Mercy felt a rush of affection for Fitzgerald.

If he asked her again she would marry him in a flash.

"HE DID, you know," Mercy said. "Save our lives."

Calvin said, "When Kit and I came out of the

woods Laurel was pumping shots into the dark. It was like a war zone.''

"She knew she'd hit Fitzgerald. She was trying to get me."

"Old Calvin," Kit said, "it was like he was playing football. You should have seen it. He came out of the woods and hit Laurel in the back with a flying tackle and she went ass over elbows. The shotgun landed ten yards away."

"All I could think of was Brand," Mercy said. "I thought he was there, too, and he'd start shooting."

"Naw," Kit said, "Calvin and me had fixed him. We'd left him up a creek without a paddle."

Calvin said, "The deputies that went out there, after they hunted down Brand, I told them to find my canoes. My fishing hat's in the one."

"You know," Mercy said, "while Laurel was talking I understood about Rawlings. Why the wire, the way it was fixed to the trees, stuck in his mind. Link and Brand did it in a hurry because they didn't plan on it working. They weren't trying to kill anyone. They just wanted Verlyn in trouble. But it worked well enough to kill Link."

"Some jerk," Kit said, "taking himself out that way."

"We'll never know what actually happened that morning. Rawlings saw the wire first, the sunlight on it. Maybe when we jumped out of our cover and started shouting, Link got disoriented. He didn't expect that. He expected us to stay hidden until he started cutting the sweeper. I remember he looked up, looked our way, just before he hit the wire.''

"What I don't get," Kit said, "is Laurel and Brand. Why did they get so uptight about Link?"

"Ossning's a small town. People talk."

"So what?"

"They talk behind your back, point fingers. Laurel and Brand couldn't stand the humiliation of the town knowing Link had caused his own death. I know, it sounds loony. But that's the way it is around here."

"So move to Detroit."

"Could you?" Then Mercy said, "Life's complicated. You don't have as many options as you think. You'll find out."

"YOU KNOW SOMETHING?" Calvin said. "I don't know Fitzgerald's name."

"Donal," Mercy said. "I had to tell them at the hospital."

"Funny name."

"Irish, I think. He used initials when he worked for the *Free Press*."

"I can understand that."

"So's Calvin, a funny name."

"I was thinking of Mercy."

"It doesn't fit me? That's what you mean?"

She was getting ready for Calvin's reply when she noticed Nils and Wilma putting on their coats to leave. When she waved goodbye to them Wilma came down the bar and said Sandy had told them about Fitzgerald. She and Nils were worried.

"He'll be fine," Mercy said.

"But he's in the hospital."

"Only for a few days." Then Mercy said, "If you visit him, Wilma, I'm sure he'll give you numbers."

"That's good."

Mercy smiled. "Isn't it, though."

HARVEST OF BONES
A VERMONT MYSTERY

NANCY MEANS WRIGHT

Ruth Willmarth, busy working to keep her rural Vermont dairy farm in a manageable state, is plunged into a mystery. It starts with a finger bone, and leads to a skeleton.

New neighbor Fay Hubbard has just opened a farmhouse B&B and finds her home invaded by its original owner, a gutsy septuagenarian who announces the dead body is that of her husband—whom she murdered twenty years ago.

The bizarre discovery puts Ruth and Fay in the middle of a twisted history of hatred, blackmail and murder, as deep and dark as the rich Vermont soil.

Available October 1999 at your favorite retail outlet.

WORLDWIDE LIBRARY®